Apart from enjoying an enviable reputation as one of the best writers on the science fiction scene, Harry Harrison is a man of wide interests and accomplishments.

A first class short story writer, an experienced editor and anthologist (compiler, with Brian Aldiss, of Sphere's *Year's Best SF* series), a translator (from Danish and Italian), a trained cartoonist, he has also been a commercial illustrator, hydraulic press operator, truck driver and is, of course, a first rate novelist.

Harrison's style leaps from the humour of his *Stainless Steel Rat* novels to purist sf to the splendid combination of fantasy and science fiction found in *Captive Universe*.

*Also by Harry Harrison and available from Sphere Books*

NOVA 1 - 2
THE STAINLESS STEEL RAT
THE STAINLESS STEEL RAT'S REVENGE
CAPTIVE UNIVERSE
THE JUPITER LEGACY
DEATHWORLD 1 - 3
YEAR'S BEST SCIENCE FICTION 1 - 7 (co-editor with Brian Aldiss)
THE ASTOUNDING-ANALOG READER 1 - 2 (co-editor with Brian Aldiss)

# The Stainless Steel Rat Saves the World

**HARRY HARRISON**

SPHERE BOOKS LIMITED
30/32 Gray's Inn Road, London WC1X 8JL

First published in Great Britain by Faber and Faber Ltd 1973
Copyright © Harry Harrison 1972
Published by Sphere Books 1975

TRADE
MARK

Set in Monotype Baskerville

Printed in Great Britain by
Hazell Watson & Viney Ltd
Aylesbury, Bucks

ONE

'You are a crook, James Bolivar diGriz,' Inskipp said, making animal noises deep in his throat while shaking the sheaf of papers viciously in my direction. I leaned back against the sideboard in his office, a picture of shocked sincerity.

'I am innocent,' I sobbed. 'A victim of a campaign of cold, calculating lies.' I had his humidor behind my back and by touch alone – I really am good at this sort of thing – I felt for the lock.

'Embezzlement, swindling and worse – the reports are still coming in. You have been cheating your own organization, our Special Corps, your own buddies—'

'Never!' I cried, lockpick busy in my fingers.

'They don't call you Slippery Jim for nothing!'

'A mistake, a childish nickname. As a baby my mother found me slippery when she soaped me in the bath.' The humidor sprang open, and my nose twitched at the aroma of fragrant leaf.

'Do you know how much you have stolen?' His face was bright red now, and his eyes were beginning to bulge in a highly unattractive manner.

'Me? Steal? I would rather die first!' I declaimed movingly as I slipped out a handful of the incredibly expensive cigars destined for visiting VIP's. I could put them to a far more important use by smoking them myself. I am forced to admit that my attention was more on the purloined tobacco than on Inskipp's tedious complaints so I did not at first notice the change in his voice. Then I suddenly realized that I could barely hear his words – not that I really wanted to in any case. It wasn't that he was whispering; it was more as though there were a volume control in his throat that had suddenly been turned down.

'Speak up, Inskipp,' I told him firmly. 'Or are you sud-

5

denly beset with guilt over these false accusations?'

I stepped away from the sideboard, half turning as I moved in order to mask the fact that I was slipping about 100 credits' worth of exotic tobacco into my pocket. He rattled on weakly, ignoring me, shaking the papers soundlessly now.

'Aren't you feeling well?'

I asked this with a certain amount of real concern because he was beginning to sound rather distant. He did not turn his head to look at me when I moved but instead kept staring at the place where I had been, nattering away in an inaudible voice. And he was looking pale. I blinked and looked again.

Not pale, transparent.

The back of his chair was very definitely becoming visible through his head.

'Stop it!' I shouted, but he did not appear to hear. 'What games are you playing? Is this some sort of three-D projection to fool me? Why bother? Slippery Jim's not the kind who can be fooled, ha-ha!'

Walking quickly across the room, I put out my hand and poked my index finger into his forehead. It went in – there was slight resistance – and he did not seem to mind in the least. But when I withdrew it, there was a slight popping sound and he vanished completely while the sheaf of papers, now unsupported, fell to the desktop.

'*Whargh!*' I grunted, or something equally incomprehensible. I bent to look for hidden devices under the chair when, with a very nasty crunching sound, the office door was broken down.

Now this was something I could understand. I whirled about, still in the crouch, and was ready for the first man when he came through the door. The hard edge of my hand got him in the throat, right under the gas mask, and he gurgled and dropped. But there were plenty more behind him, all with masks and white coats, wearing little black packs on their backs, either barefisted or carrying improvised clubs. It was all very unusual. Weight of numbers forced me back, but I caught one of them under the chin with my toe

6

while a hard jab to the solar plexus polished off another. Then I had my shoulders to the wall, and they began to swarm over me. I smashed one of them across the back of the neck, and he fell. And vanished halfway to the floor.

This was very interesting. The number of people in the room began to change rapidly now as some of the men I hit snuffed out of sight. This was a good thing that helped even the odds except for the fact that others kept appearing out of thin air at about the same rate. I struggled to get to the door, could not make it, then the club got me in the side of the head and scrambled my brains nicely.

After that it was like trying to fight slow motion under water. I hit a few more of them, but my heart wasn't really in it. They had my arms and legs and began to drag me from the room. I writhed about a certain amount and cursed them fluently in a half dozen languages, but all of this had just about the results you would expect. They rushed me from the room and down the corridor and into the waiting elevator. One of them held up a canister, and I tried to turn my head away, but the blast of gas caught me full in the face.

It did nothing for me that I could feel, though I did get angrier. Kicking and snapping my teeth and shouting insults. The masked men mumbled back in what might have been irritated mumbles, which only goaded me to greater fury. By the time we reached our destination I was ready to kill, which I normally do not find easy to do, and certainly would have if I hadn't been strapped into a gadgety electric chair and had electrodes fastened to my wrists and ankles.

'Tell them that Jim diGriz died like a man, you dogs!' I shouted, not without a certain amount of slavering and foaming. A metal helmet was lowered over my head, and just before it covered my face I managed to call out, 'Up the Special Corps! And up your—'

Darkness descended, and I was aware that death or electrocution or brain destruction or worse was imminent.

Nothing happened, and the helmet was raised again, and one of the attackers gave me another shot in the face from a canister, and I felt the overwhelming anger draining away as fast as it had arrived. I blinked a bit at this and saw that they were freeing my arms and legs. I also saw that most of them had their masks off now and were recognizable as the Corps technicians and scientists who usually puttered about this lab.

'Someone wouldn't like to tell me just what the hell is going on, would they?'

'Let me fix this first,' one of them said, a gray-haired man with buckteeth like old yellowed gravestones caught between his lips. He hung one of the black boxes from my shoulder and pulled a length of wire from it that had a metal button on the end. He touched the button to the back of my neck where it stuck.

'You're Professor Coypu, aren't you?'

'I am.' The teeth moved up and down like piano keys.

'Would you think me rude if I asked for an explanation?'

'Not at all. Only natural under the circumstances. Terribly sorry we had to rough you up. Only way. Get you off-balance, keep you angry. The angry mind exists only for itself and can survive by itself. If we had tried to reason, to tell you the problem, we would have defeated our own purpose. So we attacked. Gave you the anger gas as well as breathed it ourselves. Only thing to do. Oh blast, there goes Magistero. It's getting stronger even in here.'

One of the white-coated men shimmered and grew transparent, then vanished.

'Inskipp went that way,' I said.

'He would. First to go, you know.'

'Why?' I asked, smiling warmly, thinking that this was the most idiotic conversation I had ever had.

'They are after the Corps. Pick off the top people first.'

'Who?'

'Don't know.'

I heard my teeth grating together but managed to keep my temper. 'Would you kindly explain in greater detail or find someone who can make more sense of this affair than you have been doing.'

'Sorry. My fault entirely.' He dabbed at a beading of sweat on his forehead, and a whisk of red tongue dampened the dry ends of his teeth. 'It all came about so fast, you know. Emergency measures, everything. Time war, I imagine one might call it. Someone, somewhere, somewhen, is tampering with time. Naturally they had to pick the Special Corps as their first target, no matter what other ambitions they might have. Since the Corps is the most effective, most widespread supranational and supraplanetal law enforcement organization in the history of the galaxy, we automatically become the main obstacle in their path. Sooner or later in any ambitious time-changing plan they run up against the Corps. They have therefore elected to do it soonest. If they can eliminate Inskipp and the other top people, the probability of the Corps' existence will be lowered and we'll all snuff out, as poor Magistero did just then.'

I blinked rapidly. 'Do you think we could have a drink that might act as a bit of lubricant to my thoughts?'

'Splendid idea, join you myself.'

The dispenser produced a sickly sort of green liquid that he favored, but I dialed for a large Syrian Panther Sweat, most of which I drained with the first swallow. This frightening beverage – whose hideous aftereffects forbade its sale on most civilized worlds – did me nothing but good at this moment. I finished the glass, and a sudden memory popped up out of the tangled jumble of my subconscious.

'Stop me if I'm wrong, but didn't I hear you lecture once about the impossibility of time travel?'

'Of course. My specialty. Smoke screen that talk, I think you might call it. We've had time travel for years here. Afraid to use it, though. Alter time tracks and all that sort of trouble. Just the kind of thing that is happening now. But we have had a continuing project of research and time investigation. Which is why we knew what was happening when it began to happen. The alarms were going off, and we had no time to warn anyone – not that warnings would do any good. We were aware of our duty. Plus the fact that we were the only ones who could do anything at all. We jury-rigged a time-fixator around this laboratory, then made the smaller portable models such as the one you are wearing now.'

'What does it do?' I asked, touching with great respect the metal disk on the nape of my neck.

'Has a recording of your memory that it keeps feeding back to your brain every three milliseconds. Telling you you are you, you see, rebuilding any personality changes that time line alterations in the past may have shifted. Purely a defensive mechanism, but it is all we have.' Out of the corner of my eye I saw another man wink out of sight, and the professor's voice grew grim. 'We must attack if we are to save the Corps.'

'Attack? How?'

'Send someone back in time to uncover the forces waging this time war and destroy them before they destroy us. We have a machine.'

'I volunteer. Sounds like my kind of job.'

'There is no way to return. It is a one-way mission.'

'I withdraw the last statement. I like it here.' Sudden memory – restored no doubt three milliseconds earlier – grabbed me and a prod of fear pumped a number of interesting chemical substances into my blood.

'Angelina, *my* Angelina! I must speak to her. . . .'

'She is not the only one!'

'The only one for me, Prof. Now stand aside or I'll go through you.'

He stepped back, frowning and mumbling and tapping his teeth with his fingernails, and I jabbed the code into the phone. The screen beeped twice, and the few seconds crawled by like lead snails before she answered the call.

'You're there!' I gasped.

'Where did you expect me to be?' A frown crossed her perfect features, and she sniffed as though to get the aroma of booze from the screen. 'You've been drinking, and so early too.'

'Just a drop, but that's not why I called. How are you?

You look good, great, not transparent at all.'

'A drop? Sounds more like a whole bottle.' Her voice chilled, and there was more than a trace left of the old, unreformed Angelina, the most ruthless and deadly crook in the galaxy before the Corps medics straightened out the knots in her brain. 'I suggest you hang up. Get a drive-right pill, then call me back as soon as you are sober.' She reached out for the disconnect button.

'*Don't!* I am cold sober and wish I weren't. This is an emergency, red A top priority. Get over here now as absolutely fast as you can and bring the twins.'

'Of course.' She was on her feet instantly, ready to go. 'Where are you?'

'The location of this lab, quick!' I said, turning to Professor Coypu.

'Level one-hundred and twelve. Room thirty.'

'Did you get that,' I said, turning back to the screen.

Which was blank.

'*Angelina. . . .*'

I jabbed the disconnect, tapped her code on the keys. The screen lit up. With the message 'This is an unconnected number.' Then I ran for the door. Someone clutched at my shoulder, but I brushed him aside, grabbed the door and flung it open.

There was nothing outside. A formless, colorless nothing that did strange things to my brain when I looked at it. Then the door was pulled from my hand and slammed shut, and Coypu stood with his back to it, breathing heavily, his features twisted by the same unnamable sensations I had felt.

'Gone,' he said hoarsely. 'The corridor, the entire station, all the buildings, everything. Gone. Just this laboratory left, locked here by the time-fixator. The Special Corps no longer exists; no one in the galaxy has even a memory of us. When the time-fixator goes we go as well.'

'Angelina, where is she, where are they all?'

'They were never born, never existed.'

'But I can remember her, all of them.'

'That is what we count upon. As long as there is one person alive with memories of us, of the Corps, we stand a microscopic chance of eventual survival. Someone must stop the time attack. If not for the Corps, for the sake of civilization. History is now being rewritten. But not forever if we can counterattack.'

A one-way trip backward to a lifetime on an alien world, in an alien time. Whoever went would be the loneliest man alive, living thousands of years before his people, his friends, would even be born.

'Get ready,' I said. 'I'll go.'

# TWO

'First we must find out where you are going. And when.'

Professor Coypu staggered across the laboratory, and I followed, in almost as bad shape. He was mumbling over the accordion sheets of the computer print-out that were chuntering and pouring out of the machine and piling up on the floor.

'Must be accurate, very accurate,' he said. 'We have been running a time probe backward. Following the traces of these disturbances. We have found the particular planet. Now we must zero in on the time. If you arrive too late, they may have already finished their job. Too early and you might die of old age before the fiends are even born.'

'Sounds charming. What is the planet?'

'Strange name. Or rather names. It is called Dirt or Earth or something like that. Supposed to be the legendary home of all mankind.'

'Another one? I never heard of it.'

'No reason you should. Blown up in an atomic war ages ago. Here it is. You have to be pushed backward thirty-two thousand five hundred and ninety-eight years. We can't guarantee anything better than a plus or minus three months at that distance.'

'I don't think I'll notice. What year will that be?'

'Well before our present calendar began. It is, I believe, A.D. 1975 by the primitive records of the aborigines of the time.'

'Not so aboriginal if they're fiddling with time travel.'

'Probably not them at all. Chances are the people you are looking for are just operating in that period.'

'How do I find them?'

'With this.' One of the assistants handed me a small black box with dials and buttons on it, as well as a transparent bulge that contained a free-floating needle. The needle quivered like a hunting dog and continued to point in the same direction no matter how I turned the box.

'A detector of temporal energy generators,' Coypu said. 'A less sensitive and portable version of our larger machines. Right now it is pointing at our time-helix. When you return to this planet Dirt, you will use it to seek out the people you want. This other dial is for field strength and will give you an approximation of the distance to the energy source.'

I looked at the box and felt the first bubbling and seething of an idea. 'If I can carry this, I can take other equipment with me, right?'

'Correct. Small items that can be secured close to your body. The time field generates a surface charge that is not unlike static electricity.'

'Then I'll take whatever weapons or armament you have here in the lab.'

'There is not very much, just the smaller items.'

'Then I'll make my own. Are there any weapons technicians working here?'

He looked around and thought. 'Old Jarl there was in the weapons sections. But there is no time to fabricate anything.'

'That's not what I had in mind. Get him.'

Old Jarl had taken his rejuvenation treatments recently so he looked like a world-soiled nineteen-year-old – with an ancient and suspicious look in his eye as he came closer.

'I want that box,' I said, pointing to the memory unit on his back. He whinnied like a prodded pony and skittered away, clutching at the thing.

'Mine, I tell you mine! You can't have it. Not fair to even ask. Without it I'll just fade away.' Tears of senile self-pity rose to his youthful eyes.

'Control yourself, Jarl! I don't want to fade you out; I just want a duplicate of the box. Get cracking on it.'

He shambled away, mumbling to himself, and the technicians closed in.

'I don't understand,' Coypu said.

'Simple. If I am gunning after a large organization, I may need some heavy weapon. If I do, I'll plug old Jarl into my brain and use his memories to build them.'

'But – he will be *you*, take over your body, it has never been done.'

'It's being done now. Desperate times demand desperate measures. Which brings us to another important point. You said this would be a one-way trip through time and that I couldn't return.'

'Yes. The time-helix hurls you into the past. There will be no helix there to return you.'

'But if one could be built there, I could return?'

'Theoretically. But it has never been tried. Much of the equipment and materials would not be available among the primitive natives.'

'But if the materials were available, a time-helix *could* be built. Now who do you know that could build it?'

'Only myself. The helix is of my own construction and design.'

'Great, I'll want your memory box, too. Be sure you boys paint your names on the outside so I don't hook up with the wrong specialist.'

The technicians grabbed for the professor.

'The time-fixator is losing power!' one of the engineers shouted in a voice filled with rising hysteria. 'When the field goes down, we die. We will never have existed. It can't be. . . .' He screamed this, then fell over as one of his mates gave him a faceful of knockout gas.

'Hurry!' Coypu shouted. 'Take diGriz to the time-helix, prepare him!'

They grabbed me and rushed me into the next room, shouting instructions at one another. They almost dropped me when two of the technicians vanished at the same moment. Most of the voices had hysterical overtones – as well they might with the world coming to an end. Some of the more distant walls were already becoming misty and vague. Only training and experience kept me from panicking too. I finally had to push them away from the emergency space suit they were trying to jam me into in order to close the fastenings myself. Professor Coypu was the only other cool one in the whole crowd.

'Seat the helmet, but leave the faceplate open until the last minute. That's fine. Here are the memories, I suggest the leg pocket would be the safest place. The grav-chute on your back. I assume you know how to operate it. These weapon canisters across your chest. The temporal detector here. . . .'

There was more like this until I could hardly stand. I didn't complain. If I didn't take it, I wouldn't have it. Hang on more.

'A language unit!' I shouted. 'How can I speak to the natives if I don't know their language?'

'We don't have one here,' Coypu said, tucking a rack of gas containers under my arm. 'But here is a memory-gram—'

'They give me headaches.'

'—that you can use to learn the local tongue. In this pocket.'

'What do I do, you haven't explained that yet? How do I arrive?'

'Very high. In the stratosphere, that is. Less chance of colliding with anything material. We'll get you there. After that – you're on your own.'

'The front lab is gone!' someone shouted, and popped out of existence at almost the same instant.

'To the time-helix!' Coypu called out hoarsely, and they dragged me through the door.

Slower and slower as the scientists and technicians vanished from sight like pricked balloons. Until there were only four of them left and, heavily burdened, I staggered along at a decrepit waddle.

'The time-helix,' Coypu said, breathlessly. 'It is a bar, a column of pure force that has been warped into a helix and put under tension.'

It was green and glittered and almost filled the room, a

coiled form of sparkling light as thick as my arm. It reminded me of something.

'It's like a big spring that you have wound up.'

'Yes, perhaps. We prefer to call it a time-helix. It has been wound up . . . put under tension, the force carefully calculated. You will be placed at the outer end and the restraining latch released. As you are flung into the past, the helix will hurl itself into the future where the energies will gradually dissipate. You must go.'

There were just three of us left.

'Remember me,' the short dark technician called out. 'Remember Charli Nate! As long as you remember me, I'll never . . .'

Coypu and I were alone, the walls going, the air darkening.

'The end! Touch it!' he called out. Was his voice weaker?

I stumbled, half fell toward the glowing end of the helix, my fingers outstretched. There was no sensation, but when I touched it, I was instantly surrounded by the same green glow, could barely see through it. The professor was at a console, working the controls, reaching for a rather large switch.

Pulling it down. . . .

# THREE

Everything stopped.

Professor Coypu stood frozen at the controls with his hand locked on the closed switch. I had been looking in his direction, or I would not have seen this because my eyes were fixed rigidly ahead. My body as well — and my brain gave a flutter of panic and tried to bounce around in its bony pan as I realized that I had stopped breathing. For all I knew, my heart wasn't beating either. Something had gone wrong, I was sure of that, since the time-helix was still tightly coiled. More soundless panic as Coypu grew transparent and the walls behind him took on a definitely hazy quality. It was all going, fading before my eyes. Would I be next? There was no way to know.

A primitive part of my mind, the ape-man's heir, jibbered and wailed and rushed about in little circles. Yet at the same time I felt a cold detachment and interest; it isn't everyone who is privileged to watch the dissolving of his world while hanging from a helical force field that may possibly whip him back into the remote past. It was a privilege I would be happy to pass on to any volunteers. None presented themselves, so I hung there, popeyed and stiff as a statue while the laboratory faded away around me and I was floating in interstellar space. Apparently even the asteroid on which the Special Corps base had been built no longer had any reality in this new universe.

Something moved. I was tugged in a way that is impossible to describe and moved in a direction I never knew existed before. The time-helix was beginning to uncoil. Or perhaps it had been uncoiling all the while and the alteration in time had concealed my awareness of it. Certainly some of the stars appeared to be moving, faster and faster until they made little blurred lines. It was not a reassuring sight, and I tried to close my eyes, but the paralysis still clutched me. A star whipped by, close enough so that I could see its disk, and burned an afterimage across my retina. Everything speeded up as my time speed accelerated, and eventually space became a gray blur as even stellar events became too fast for me to see. This blur had a hypnotic effect, or my brain was affected by the time motion, because my thoughts became thoroughly muddled as I sank into a quasi-state somewhere between sleep and unconsciousness that lasted a very long time. Or a short time, I'm not really sure. It could have been an instant, or it could have been eternity. Perhaps there was some corner of my brain that remained aware of the terrible slow passage of all those years, but if so, I do not care to think about it. Survival has always been rather important to me, and as a stainless steel rat in among the concrete passages of society I look only to myself for aid. There are far more ways to fail than to succeed, to go mad than to stay sane, and I needed all my mental energies to find the right course. So I existed and stayed relatively sane during the insane temporal voyage and waited for something to happen. After an immeasurable period of time something did.

I arrived. The ending was even more dramatic than the beginning of the journey as everything happened all at once.

I could move again. I could see again – the light blinded me at first – and I was aware of all the bodily sensations that had been suspended so long.

More than that, I was falling. My long-paralyzed stomach gave a twist at this, and the adrenalin and like substances that my brain had been longing to pour into my blood for the past 32,598 years – give or take three months – pumped in and my heart began to thud in a healthily excited manner. As I fell, I turned, and the sun was out of my eyes, and I looked out at a black sky and down at fluffy white clouds far below. Was this it? Dirt, the mysterious homeland of mankind? There was no telling, but it was still a distinct pleasure to be somewhere and somewhen without things dissolving around me. All my equipment seemed to still be with me, and when

I touched the control on my wrist, I could feel the tug of the grav-chute taking hold. Great. I turned it off and dropped free again until I felt the first traces of thin atmosphere pulling at the suit. By the time I came to the clouds I was falling gently as a leaf, plunging feetfirst into their wet embrace. I slowed the rate of fall even more as I dropped blind, rubbing at the condensation on the faceplate of the space suit. Then I was out of the clouds, and I turned the control to *hover* and took a slow look around at this new world, perhaps the home of the human race, surely my home forever.

Above me the clouds hung like a soft wet ceiling. There were trees and countryside about 3,000 meters below with the details blurred by my wet faceplate. I had to try the atmosphere here sooner or later, and hoping my remote ancestors were not methane breathers, I cracked the faceplate and took a quick sniff.

Not bad. Cold and a little thin at this height, but sweet and fresh. And it didn't kill me. I opened the faceplate wide, breathed deeply, and looked down at the world below. Pleasant enough from this altitude. Rolling green hills covered with trees of some kind, blue lakes, roads cutting sharply through the valleys, some sort of city on the horizon boiling out clouds of pollution. I'd stay as far away from that as possible for the time being. I had to establish myself first, see about . . .

The sound had been pushing at my awareness, a thin humming like an insect. But there shouldn't be insects at this altitude. I would have thought of this sooner if my attention hadn't been on the landscape below. Just about the time I realized this the humming grew to a roar and I twisted to look over my shoulder. Gaping. At the globular flying craft supported by an archaic rotating airfoil of some kind, behind the transparent sides of which there sat a man gaping back at me. I slammed the wrist controller to *lift* and shot back up into the protecting cloud.

Not a very good beginning. The pilot had had a very good look at me, although there was always the chance that he might disbelieve what he saw. He didn't. The communicators in this age must be most sophisticated, the military's preparedness or paranoia equally so, because within a few minutes I heard the rumble of powerful jets below. They circled a bit, roaring and bellowing, and one even shot up through the clouds. I had a quick glimpse of an arrowlike silver form; then it was gone, the clouds roiling and seething in its wake. It was time to leave. The lateral control on a grav-chute isn't too precise, but I wobbled off through the clouds to put as much room between myself and those machines as I could. When I had not heard them for some time, I risked a drop down just below the cloud level. Nothing. In any direction. I snapped my faceplate shut and cut all the power.

The drop in free fall could not have taken very long, though it seemed a lot longer. I had unhealthy visions of detectors clattering, computers digesting the information and pointing mechanical fingers, mighty machines of war whistling and roaring toward me. I rotated as I fell, squinting my eyes for the first sight of shining metal.

Nothing at all happened. Some large white birds flapped slowly along, veering off with sharp squawks as I plunged by. There was the blue mirror of a lake below, and I gave a nudge of power that moved me toward it. If the pursuit did show up, I could drop under the surface and out of detection range. When I was below the level of the surrounding hills with the water rushing up uncomfortably close below, I slammed on the power. I shuddered and groaned and felt the straps cutting deep into my flesh. The grav-chute on my back grew uncomfortably warm, though I began to sweat for a different reason. It was still a long fall, to water hard as steel from this height.

When I finally did stop moving, my feet were in the water. Not a bad landing at all. There was still no sign of pursuit as I lifted a bit above the surface and drifted toward the gray cliff that fell directly into the lake on the far side. The air smelled good when I opened the faceplate again, and everything was silent. No voices, no sounds of machines. Nor signs of human habitation. When I came closer to the shore, I heard the wind in the leaves, but that was all. Great. I needed a place to hole up until I got my bearings, and this would do just fine. The gray cliff turned out to be a wall of solid rock, inaccessible and high. I drifted along its face until I found a ledge wide enough to sit on, so I sat. It felt good.

'Been a long time since I sat down,' I said aloud, pleased to hear my voice. *Yeah,* my evil subconscious snapped back *about thirty-three thousand years.* I was depressed again and wished that I had a drink. But that was the one essential supply I had neglected to bring, a mistake I would have to rectify quickly. With the power cut the space suit began to warm up in the sun, and I stripped it off, placing all the items of equipment against the rock far from the edge.

What next? I felt something crunch in my side pocket and pulled out a handful of hideously expensive and broken cigars. A tragedy. By some miracle one of them was intact, so I snapped the end to ignite it and breathed deep. Wonderful! I smoked for a bit, my legs dangling over the drop below, and let my morale build up to its normal highly efficient level. A fish broke through the surface of the lake and splashed back; some small birds twittered in the trees, and I thought about the next step. I needed shelter, but the more I moved around to find it, the more chance I had of being discovered. Why couldn't I stay right here?

Among the assorted junk I had been draped with at the last minute was a laboratory tool called a masser. I had started to complain at the time, but it was hung on my waist before I could say anything. I considered it now. The handgrip that contained the power source blossomed out into a bulbous body, which thinned again into a sharp, spikelike prod. A field was generated at the end that had the interesting ability of being able to concentrate most forms of matter by increasing the binding energy in the molecules. This would crunch them together into a smaller space, though they of course still had the same mass. Some things, depending upon the material and the power used, could be compressed up to one-half their original size.

At the other end the ledge narrowed until it vanished, and I walked along it as far as I safely could. Reaching out, I pressed the spike to the surface of the gray stone and thumped the button. There was a sharp crack as a compressed slab of stone the size of my hand fell from the face of the cliff and slid down to the ledge. It felt heavy, more like lead than rock. Flipping it out into the lake, I turned up the power and went to work.

Once I got the knack of the thing the job went fast. I found I could generate an almost spherical field that would detach a solid ball of compressed stone as big as my head. After I had struggled to roll a couple of these heavyweights over the edge – and almost rolled myself with them – I worked the rock away at an angle, then cut out above this slope. The spheres would crunch free, bang down onto the slope, and roll off the edge in a short arc, to splash noisily into the water below. Every once in a while I would stop and listen and look. I was still alone. The sun was close to the horizon before I had a neat little cave in the rock face that would just hold all my goods and myself. An animal's den that I longed to crawl into. Which I did, after a quick floating trip down to the lake for some water. The concentrates were tasteless but filling, so my stomach knew that I had dined, though not well. As the first stars began to come out, I planned the next step in my conquest of Dirt, or Earth, whichever the name was.

My time voyage must have been more fatiguing than I had thought because the next thing I realized was that the sky was black and a great orange full moon was sitting on the mountains. My bottom was chilled from contact with the cold rock, and I was stiff from sleeping in a cramped sitting position.

'Come, mighty changer of history,' I said, and groaned as my muscles creaked and my joints cracked. 'Get out and get to work.'

That was just what I had to do. Action would bring reaction. As long as I holed up in this den, any planning I might do would be valueless since I had no facts to operate with. As yet I didn't even know if this was the right world, or the right time – or anything else. I had to get out and get cracking. Though there was one thing I could do – that I should have done first thing upon arrival. Mumbling curses at my own stupidity, I dug through the assorted junk I had brought with me and came up with the black box of the time energy detector. I used a small light to illuminate it, and my heart thudded down on top of my stomach when I saw that the needle was floating limply. Time was not being warped anywhere on this world.

'Ha-ha, you moron,' I called out loudly, cheered by the sound of the voice I liked the most. 'This thing would work a lot better if you turned on the power.' An oversight. Taking a deep breath, I threw the switch.

Still nothing. The needle hung as limp as my deflated hopes. There was still a good chance that the time triflers were around and just happened to have their machine turned off at the present moment. I hoped.

To work. I secreted a few handy devices about my person and disengaged the grav-chute from the space suit. It still had about a half charge in its power pack, which should get me up and down the cliff a number of times. I slipped my arms through the straps, stepped off the ledge, and touched the controls so that my free fall changed to an arc that pointed in the direction of the nearest road I had seen on the way down. Floating low over the trees, I checked landmarks and direction constantly. The outsize and gleamingly be-dialed watch I always wear on my left wrist does a lot more things than tell the time. A touch of the right button illuminated the needle of the radio compass that was zeroed in on my home base. I drifted silently on.

Moonlight reflected from the smooth surface that cut a swath through the forest, and I floated down through the trees to the ground. Enough light filtered through the boughs so that I didn't need my flash as I made my way to the road, going the last few meters with extreme caution. It was empty in both directions, and the night was silent. I bent and examined the surface. It was made of a single slab of some hard white substance, not metal or plastic, that appeared to have tiny grains of sand in it. Most uninteresting. Staying close to the edge, I turned in the direction of the city I had glimpsed and started walking. It was slow, but it saved the power in the grav-chute.

What happened next I can attribute only to carelessness, tempered with fatigue, and seasoned by my ignorance of this world. My mind wandered, to Angelina and the children and my friends in the Corps, all of whom existed only in my thoughts. They now had no more reality than my memory of characters I had read about in a novel. This was a very depressing idea, and I brooded over it rather than rejected it, so I was taken completely unaware by the sudden roar of engines. At this moment I was rounding a turn in the road that had apparently been cut through a small hill, since there were steep banks on each side. I should have considered being caught in this cut and have planned some means to avoid it. Now, while I considered the advisability of climbing the slope, of lifting up by grav-chute or of some other means of escape, bright lights shone around the turn ahead and the roar grew louder. In the end I only dropped to one side of the road, in the ditch that ran there, and lay down and tried to think small, burying my face in my arm. My clothing was a neutral dark gray and might blend into the ground.

Then the stuttering roar was upon me, next to me, and bright lights washed over me and were gone. As soon as they were by, I sat up and looked after the four strange vehicles that had passed. Details were not clear, since I saw them only as silhouettes against their own headlights, but they seemed very narrow, like monocycles, and each had a little red light at the back. Their sound quieted and was mixed with a kind of honking like some animal and a shrill screeching. They were slowing. They must have seen me.

Cracking, barking sounds echoed in the cut as the lights turned full circle and headed back in my direction.

# FOUR

When in doubt, let the other guy make the first mistake, one of my older mottoes. I could attempt to escape, climbing or floating, but whoever these people were, they might have weapons, and I would make a peachy target. Even if I did escape, I would only draw attention to this area. Better to see who and what they were first. Turning my back so their lights wouldn't blind me, I waited patiently as the machines rumbled up and stopped in an arc around me, motors coughing and lights pointed at me. I closed my eyes to slits to shield them from the glare and listened to the strange sounds the riders made gabbling to one another, not one word of which I found comprehensible. The chances were good that my clothing was on the exotic side as far as they were concerned. They must have reached some agreement because the engine on one of the invisible conveyances clattered into silence and the driver stepped forward into the light.

We exchanged looks of mutual interest. He was a little shorter than I but looked taller because of the bucket-shaped metal helmet he was wearing. It was studded with rivets and bore a tall spike on the top, very unattractive, as was the rest of his dress. All black plastic with shining knobs and clasps, brought to the acme of vulgarity by a stylized skull and crossbones on the chest that was picked out with fake gems of some kind.

'*Kryzl prtzblk?*' he said in a very insulting manner, allowing his jaw to protrude at the same time. I smiled to show that I was a friendly, good-natured fellow and responded in the warmest fashion.

'You'll look uglier dead than alive, bowb, and that's what you will be if you keep talking to me that way.'

He looked puzzled at that and there was more incomprehensible chitchat back and forth. The first driver was joined by one of the others, equally strangely garbed, who pointed excitedly to my arm. All of them looked at my wrist chronometer, and there were shrill cries of interest that changed to anger when I put my hand behind my back.

'*Prubl!*' the first thug said, stepping forward with his hand out. There was a sharp snick, and a gleaming blade appeared in his other fist.

Now this was language I understood, and I almost smiled at the sight. No honest men these, unless the law of the land decreed drawing weapons on strangers and attempting to rob them. Now that I knew the rules I could play by them.

'Prubl, prubl?' I cried, shrinking away and raising my hands in a gesture of despair.

'*Prubl drubl!*' the evilly grinning lout shouted, jumping toward me.

'How's that for prubl?' I asked as I kicked up and caught him on the wrist with my toe. The knife sailed away into the darkness, and he squeaked with pain, the squeak turning into a vanishing gurgle as my pointed fingers stabbed him in the throat.

By this time all the eyes must be on me, so I triggered a miniflare into my hand from my sleeve holdout and dropped it on the ground before me, closing my eyes just before it exploded. The glare burned hot on my lids, and I saw little floating blobs of light when I opened them again. Which was a lot better than my attackers, who were all temporarily blinded if their groans and complaints meant anything. None of them stopped me as I walked behind them and gave them, each in turn, a sharp boot toe where it would do the most good. They all yiped with pain and ran in little circles until two collided by chance and began to beat each other unmercifully. While they were amusing themselves in this manner, I examined their conveyances. Strange things with only two wheels and no sign of a gyro to stabilize them in motion. Each had a single seat on which the operator sat, straddling the thing to make it go. They looked very dangerous, and I had no desire at all to learn to operate one.

What was I to do with these creatures? I had never enjoyed killing people, so they couldn't be silenced that way. If they were the criminals they appeared to be, there was a good chance they would not report the event to the authorities. Criminals! Of course, just the kind of informants I needed. One would be enough, the first one preferably since I would have no compunction about being stern with him. He was moaning his way back to consciousness, but a whiff of sleepgas put him well under. Around his waist was a wide, metal-studded belt that looked fairly strong. I fastened this to one of my belt clips and held him in friendly embrace under the arms. Then thumbed the grav-chute control.

Silently and smoothly we lifted, floating up and away from the noisy little group, arrowing back toward my lakeside retreat. Their companion's vanishing act would be singularly mysterious, and even if they reported it to the authorities, it would accomplish nothing. I was going to hole up with my dozing companion for a few days and learn the speech of this land. My accent was sure to be of the lowest, but that could be corrected later. My retreat gaped its welcoming mouth at me, and I zipped in, dropping my limp burden ungracefully on the stone.

By the time he came groaning back to awareness I was completely prepared and had all the equipment laid out. I puffed pleasurably on a cigar from my pocket humidor and said nothing while he went through a painful series of adjustments. There was plenty of lip smacking before he opened his eyes and sat up – only to moan and clutch at his head. My sleepgas does have some painful aftereffects. But memory of his knife aimed at me did much to steel me to his suffering. Then came the wild look around, the eye boggling at me and my equipment, the crafty look at the black opening of the entrance and the apparently accidental way he got his legs beneath him. To spring out of the opening. To land smash on his face as the cable that secured his ankle to the rock brought him down.

'Now the games are over and we get to work,' I told him,

not unkindly as I sat him back against the wall and tightened the device about his wrist. I had rigged it while he slept, and it was simple but effective. It contained a blood pressure and skin resistance gauge with readouts on the control box that I held before me. A basic form of lie detector. It also contained a negative reinforcement circuit. I normally wouldn't use this technique on a human being – it was usually reserved for training laboratory animals – but this present human being was an exception. We were playing by his rules, and this shortcut would save a lot of time. When he began shouting, what I am sure were obnoxious insults, and started to tear at the box, I pressed the reinforcement button. He shrieked and thrashed about enthusiastically as the electric current hit him. It wasn't really that bad; I had tried it on myself and set the level at slightly painful, the sort of pain one could easily endure but would prefer not to.

'Now we begin,' I said, 'but let me prepare myself first.'

He looked on in wide-eyed silence while I adjusted the metal pads of the memorygram on my temples and activated the circuit.

'The key word is' – I looked at my companion – 'ugly. Now we begin.'

There was a pile of simple objects at my side, and I picked up the first one and held it out before me so he could see it. When he looked at it, I said 'rock' loudly, then was silent. He was silent as well, and after a moment I triggered the reinforcement circuit and he jumped at the sudden burst of pain and looked around wildly.

'Rock,' I repeated in a quiet, patient voice.

It took him a while to get the idea, but he learned. There was a shock for cursing or saying anything irrelevant and a double shock when he tried to lie about a word; my polygraph kept me informed about that. He had enough of this quite quickly and found it easier to supply the word I wanted. We quickly ran through my supply of objects and shifted to drawings and acted-out motions. I accepted the phrase 'I don't know,' as long as it wasn't used too often, and my store of words grew. Under the pressure of the microcurrents of the memorygram the new vocabulary was jammed into my cortex, but not without some painful side effects. When my head began to throb, I took a painpill and went on with the word games. It didn't take long to file away enough words to switch to the second part of the learning process, grammar and structure. 'What is your name?' I thought to myself and added the code word 'ugly'.

'What . . . name?' I said aloud. A very unattractive language indeed.

'Slasher.'

'Me . . . name . . . Jim.'

'Lemme go, I ain't done nuttin' to you.'

'Learn first . . . leave later. Now tell, what year?'

'What year what?'

'What year now, dum-dum?'

I repeated the question in different ways until realization of what I was asking finally penetrated the solid bone of his skull. I was beginning to sweat.

'Oh, the *year*. It's 1975. June the nineteenth, 1975.'

Right on target! Across all those centuries and millennia the time-helix had snapped me with precise accuracy. I made a mental note of thanks to Professor Coypu and the other vanished scientists, and since they lived on only in my memory, this was probably the only way to send the message. Much cheered by this information, I got on with the language lesson.

The memorygram clutched onto everything he said, organized it, and jammed it deep into my bruised synapses. I stifled a groan and took another painpill. By sunrise I felt I had enough of a command of the language to add to it by myself and switched off the machine. My companion fell over asleep and clunked his head on the rock without waking. I let him sleep and disentangled us both from the electronic equipment. After the nightlong session I was tired myself, but a stimtab took care of that. Hunger growled plaintively in my gut, and I broke out some rations. Slasher awoke soon after and shared my breakfast, eating one of the bars only after he saw me break off the end and consume it myself. I belched with satisfaction, and he echoed eructatingly. He eyed me and my equipment for some time before he made a positive statement.

'I know who you are.'

'So tell me.'

'You're from Mars, dat's what.'

'What's Mars?'

'The planet, you know.'

'Yeah, you might be right. It don't matter. You gonna do what I said, help me get some loot?'

'I told you, I'm on parole. If I'm grabbed, they'll throw the key away.'

'Don't let it bug you. Stick with me and they won't lay a finger on you. You'll be rolling in bucks. Do you have any of these bucks? I want to see what they look like.'

'No!' he said, and his hand went to a bulge in a flap of material affixed to his lower garments. By this time I could detect his simple lies without my equipment.

Sleepgas quieted him, and I worked a sort of hide envelope from his clothing that contained flimsy scraps of green paper, undoubtedly the bucks he had referred to not having. To look at them was to laugh! The cheapest copying machine could turn out duplicates of these by the barrelful – unless there were hidden means of authentification. To check I went over them with the most delicate equipment and found no trace of chemical, physical, or radioactive identification. Amazing. The paper did appear to contain short threads of some kind of substance, but a duplicator would print replicas of these on the surface which would do fine. If only I had a duplicator. Or did I have a duplicator? Toward the end there they were hanging every kind of equipment on me that they could. I rooted through the pile, and sure enough, there was a tiny desk model duplicator. It was loaded with a block of extremely dense material that was expanded in some cellular fashion inside the machine to produce a sheet of smooth white plastic on which the copies were made. After a number of adjustments I managed to reduce the quality of the plastic until it was as rough and crumpled as the bucks. Now when I touched the copy button, the machine produced a buck that appeared a duplicate of the original. The largest denomination Slasher had was a ten-buck note, and I made a number of copies of this. Of course, they all had the same serial number, but my experience has been that people never look very closely at the money they accept.

It was time to move into the next phase of my penetration of the society on this primitive planet, Earth. (I had discovered that Dirt was not correct and had another meaning altogether.) I arranged about my person the equipment I might need and left the remainder in the cave with the space suit. It would be here whenever I needed it. Slasher mumbled and snored when I floated him back across the lake and low over the trees toward the road. There was more traffic on it now during the day, I could hear the vehicles rumbling by, so I once more dropped down into the forest. Before waking Slasher, I buried the grav-chute with a radio transponder that would lead me back to it if needs be.

'What, what?' Slasher said, sitting up as soon as the antidote took effect. He looked around uncomprehendingly at the forest.

'On your hooves,' I told him. 'We gotta move out of here.'

He shambled after me, still half-asleep, though he woke up rather quickly when I ruffled the wad of money under his nose.

'How do these bucks look to you?'

'Great – but I thought you didn't have any bread?'

'I got enough food, but not enough money. So I made these. Are they OK?'

'A-OK, I never seen better.' He flipped through them with the appraising eye of the professional. 'The only way you can tell is that the numbers are all the same. This is high-class green.'

He parted with them only reluctantly. A man of little imagination and no compunction; just what I needed. The sight of the bucks seemed to have driven all fear of me from him and he actively joined in planning to obtain even more money as we trudged along the road.

'That outfit you're wearing, it's OK from a distance, like now, no one in the cars notices nuttin'. But we gotta get you some threads. There's kind of a general store foot of this hill. You wait away from the road while I go in and buy what you need. In fact, maybe we get some wheels before that; my feet are killing me. There's some kind of little factory there with a parking lot. We'll see what they're selling.'

The factory proved to be a squat, squarish building with a number of chimneys that were puffing out smoke and pollution. An assortment of multicolored vehicles were arranged to one side, and following Slasher's example, I bent low as we moved quickly to the nearest one in the outside row. When he was sure we were unobserved, my companion released a catch on a swollen purple thing, with what appeared to be a row of metal teeth at one end, and lifted a large lid. I looked in and gasped at the excessively complex and primitive propulsion engine it contained. I was indeed in the past. In response to my questions, Slasher described it as he shorted some wires that seemed to control the ignition.

'An intoinal-combustion engine we call it. Almost new, should be three hundred horses there. Climb in and we'll make tracks out of here before anybody sees us.'

I made a mental note to inquire later about the theory behind this intoinal combustion. From earlier conversation I had understood that horses were rather large quadrupeds, so perhaps it was an animal miniaturizing process to get a large number of them into the machine. But primitive as the device looked, it certainly moved quickly enough. Slasher manipulated the controls and twisted the large wheel, and we shot out onto the road and were away – apparently without being detected. I was more than satisfied to let Slasher drive while I observed this world that I had arrived on.

'Where is all the money kept? You know, like the place where they lock it up.'

'You must mean the banks. Places with thick walls, big vaults, armed guards. They got at least one in every town.'

'And the bigger the town, the bigger the bank?'

'You're catchin' on.'

'Then drive on to the nearest big town and find the biggest bank. I need plenty of bread. So we'll clean it out tonight.'

Slasher gaped in awe. 'You can't mean it! They got all kinds of alarms and stuff.'

'I laugh at their Stone Age gadgets. Just find the town, find the bank, then find some food and drink. Tonight I'll make you rich.'

In all truth I have never robbed a bank more easily or cracked a simpler crib. The establishment I selected was in the center of a city with the improbable-sounding name of Hartford. It was severely constructed of gray stone, and all the openings were covered with thick metal bars – but these defenses were negated by the fact that there were other buildings joined to the bank on both sides. A rat rarely enters by the front door. It was early evening when we set out, and Slasher was jittery and nervous despite the large quantity of low-quality alcoholic beverage he had consumed.

'We oughta wait until later,' he complained. 'There are still plenty of people in the street.'

'Just how I want it. They won't pay no attention to a couple more. Now park this heap around the corner where we planned and bring the bags.'

I carried my tools in a small case while Slasher followed me with the two large pieces of luggage we had purchased. The building ahead, on the left of the bank, was dark, and the outer door was surely locked. No trouble. I had looked at the lock earlier in the day and had determined that it presented no problem at all. The device in my left hand neutralized the alarm while I inserted the lockpick with my right. It opened so easily that Slasher did not even have to stop but went right on by me with the bags. Not a soul in the street paid us the slightest attention. A corridor led to some more locked doors, which I passed through with the same ease, until we reached an office in the rear.

'This room should share a wall with the bank. Now I'm gonna find out,' I said.

I whistled under my breath as I went to work. This was by no means my first bank robbery, and I had no intention of making it my last. Of all the varied forms of crime, bank robbery is the most satisfactory to both the individual and to society. The individual of course gets a lot of money, that goes without saying, and he benefits society by putting large amounts of cash back into circulation. The economy is stimulated, small businessmen prosper, people read about the crime with great interest, and the police have a chance to exercise their various skills. Good for all. Though I have heard foolish people complain that it hurts the bank. This is arrant nonsense. All banks are insured, so they lose nothing, while the sums involved are minuscule in the overall operation of the insuring firm, where the most that might happen is that a microscopically smaller dividend will be paid at the end of the year. Little enough price to pay for all the good caused. It was as a benefactor of mankind, not a thief, that I passed the echo sounder over the wall. A large opening on the other side; the bank without a doubt.

There were a number of cables and pipes in the wall, power and water I presumed, along with some that were obviously alarms. I marked their positions on the wall until the pattern was clear. There was one area that was free of all obstructions that I outlined.

'We go in here,' I said.

'How we gonna break the wall down?' Slasher swung between elation and fear, wanting the money, afraid he would be caught. He was obviously a petty criminal, and this was the biggest job he had ever been on.

'Not break, dum-dum,' I said, not unkindly, holding up the masser. 'We just convince it to open before us.'

Of course he had no idea what I was talking about, but sight of the gleaming instrument seemed to reassure him. I had reversed the device so instead of increasing the binding energy of molecules, it reduced their attraction close to zero. With slow precision I ran the point of the device completely over the chosen area of wall, then turned it off and stowed it away.

'Nuttin' happened,' Slasher complained.

'Somethin' will now.' I pushed the wall with my hand, and

the entire area I had prepared fell away with a soft whoosh, sliding down like so much fine dust. Which it had become. We looked through into the brightly lit interior of the bank.

We were invisible from the street when we crawled through and crept along behind the high counter where the tellers normally sat. The builders had thoughtfully put their vault in the lower depths of the building and out of sight of the street, so once down the steps, we could straighten up and go about our task in comfort. In rapid sequence I went through a pair of locked doors and a grille made of thick steel bars. Their locks and alarms were too simple to discuss. The vault door itself looked more formidable, yet proved the simplest of them all.

'Look at dat,' I called out enthusiastically. 'There is a time lock here that opens automatically sometime tomorrow.'

'I knew it,' Slasher wailed. 'Let's get out before the alarms go off. . . .'

As he ran for the stairs, I tripped him and put one foot on his chest while I explained.

'That is what they call good, dum-dum. All we have to do to open the thing is to advance the clock so it thinks it is the morning.'

'Impossible! It's sealed behind a couple of inches of steel!'

Of course, he had no way of knowing that an ordinary serviceman's manipulator is designed to work through casings of any kind. When I felt the field engage the cogs, I rotated it, and the dials whirled, and his eyes bulged – and the mechanism gave a satisfied click, and the door swung open.

'Bring da bags,' I ordered, entering the vault.

Whistling and humming gaily, we packed the two bags solid with the tightly wrapped bundles of crisp notes. Slasher closed and sealed his first, then mumbled impatiently at my slowness.

'What's da rush?' I asked him, closing the case and assembling my tools. 'You gotta take the time to do things the right way.'

As I put the last of my instruments away, I noticed a needle jump, then hold steady. Interesting. I adjusted the field strength, then stood with it in my hand and looked around. Slasher was on the other side of the vault, fumbling with some long metal boxes.

'And what are you doing?' I asked in my warmest voice.

'Takin' a shufty to see if maybe there are some jewels in these safe-deposit boxes.'

'Oh, that is what you are doing. You shoulda asked me.'

'I can do it myself.' Surly and cocksure.

'Yes, but I can do it without setting off the silent alarm to the police station.' Cold and angry. 'As you have just done.'

The blood drained from his face nicely; his hands shook so he dropped the box; then he jumped about to bend and pick up the satchel of money.

'Dum-dum yo-yo,' I snarled and booted hard in the inviting target presented. 'Now get that bag and get out of here and start the car. I'm right behind you.'

Slasher stumbled and scrambled up the stairs, and I followed more calmly after, taking a moment to close all the gates and grilles behind me in order to make things as difficult as possible for the police. They would know the bank had been entered but would not know it had been robbed until they rousted out some bank official and opened the vault. By which time we would be long vanished.

But as I came up the stairs, I heard the squeal of tires and saw, through the front windows, a police car pulling up outside.

They had certainly been fast, incredibly so for an ancient and primitive society like this one. Though perhaps that was why; certainly crime and crime detection must consume a large part of everyone's energies. However, I wasted no time philosophizing over their arrival but pushed the bags ahead of me as I crawled behind the tellers' counter. As I was going through the hole to the other building, I heard keys rattling in the outer door locks. Just right. As they came in, I would go out – and this proved to be the case. When I looked out at the street, I saw that all the occupants of the police car had entered the bank while a small, but curious, crowd had gathered. With their backs toward me. I exited slowly and strode toward the corner.

The Neolithic fuzz were certainly fast on their feet. It must come from running down and catching their own game or something. Because I had not reached the corner before they popped out of the door behind me, tooting painfully on shrill whistles. They had entered the bank, seen the hole in the wall, then retraced my path. I took one quick look at them, all shining teeth, blue uniforms, brass buttons and guns, and started running myself.

Around the corner and into the car.

Except that the street was empty and the car was gone.

Slasher must have decided that he had earned enough for one evening and had driven away and left me for the law.

# SIX

I am not suggesting that I may be made of sterner stuff than most men. Though I do feel that most men when presented with a situation like this – 32,000 years in the past, a load of stolen money, the law in hot pursuit – might give way to more than a little suggestion of panic. Only conditioning, and the fact that I had been in this position far too often during my life, kept me running smoothly while I considered what to do next. In a few moments some heavy-footed minions of the law would come barreling around the corner while, I am sure, a radio alarm would be drawing in reinforcements to cut me off. Think fast, Jim.

I did. Before I had taken five more paces, my entire plan for escape was outlined, detailed, set into type, printed, and bound into a little booklet with page one open in my mind's eye before me.

First – get off the street. As I jumped into the next door-way, I dropped the money and let a minigrenade fall into my fingers from my holdout. This fitted into the round opening of the keyhole very nicely, and with an impressive thud, it blew out the lock and part of the frame. My pursuers were not in sight yet, so I hesitated until they appeared before pushing open the ruined door. Hoarse shouts and more whistle blowing signaled that I had been observed. The door opened into a long corridor, and I was at the far end of it, hands raised in surrender, when the gun-toting law hesitatingly peeked in through the opening.

'Don't shoot, coppers,' I shouted. 'I surrender, a poor young man led to crime by evil companions.'

'Don't move or we'll hole you,' they growled happily, entering warily with strong lights flashing into my eyes. I simply stood there, fingers groping for empty air, until the lights slid away and there was the double thud of falling bodies. There should have been since there was more sleep-gas than air in that hallway.

Being careful to breathe through the filter plugs in my nostrils, I stripped the uniform from the snoring figure that was closest to my size, cursing the crude arrangement of fastenings, and put it on over my own clothes. Then I took the hand weapon he had been carrying and restored it to its holster, picked up my bags again and left, walking back up the street toward the bank. Frightened civilians peered out of doorways like animals from their burrows, and at the corner I was met by another police car. As I had guessed, a number of them were converging on this spot.

'I have the loot,' I called in to the solid figure behind the wheel. 'I'm takin it back to da bank. We have them cornered, da rats, a whole gang. Through that door. Go get them!'

This last advice was unneeded because the vehicle had already left. The first police conveyance still stood where I had last seen it, and under the cowlike eyes of the spectators, I threw the bags into the front seat and climbed in.

'Gowan, beat it. Da show's over,' I shouted as I groped among the unfamiliar instruments. There were an awful lot of them, enough to fly a spaceship with, much less this squalid groundcar. Nothing happened. The crowd milled back, then milled forward. I was sweating slightly. Only then did I notice that the tiny keyhole was empty and remembered – belatedly – something Slasher had said about using keys to start these vehicles with. Sirens grew louder on all sides as I groped and fumbled through the odd selection of pockets and wallets on the uniform I wore.

Keys! An entire ring of them. Chortling, I pushed one after another into the keyhole until I realized that they were all too big to fit. Outside, the fascinated crowd pressed close, greatly admiring my performance.

'Back, back,' I cried, and struggled the weapon from its holster to add menace to my words.

Evidently it had been primed and was ready to be actu-ated, and I inadvertently touched the wrong control. There

41

was a terrible explosion and cloud of smoke, and it jumped from my hand. Some kind of projectile hurtled through the metal roof of the car and my thumb felt quite sore.

At least the spectators left. Hurriedly. As they ran in all directions, I saw that one of the police cars was coming up behind me, and I felt that things were just not going as well as they should. There must be other keys. I groped again, throwing the miscellaneous items I discovered onto the seat beside me until there were no more. The other car stopped behind mine and the doors opened.

Was that a glint of metal in that small hide case? It was. A pair of keys. One of them slid gently into the correct orifice as the two minions of law and order walked up on both sides of the car.

'What's going on here?' the nearest called out as the key turned and there was the groaning of an engine and a metallic clashing.

'Trouble!' I said as I fumbled with the metal levers.

'Get outta there, you!' he said, pulling out his weapon.

'Matter of life and death!' I shouted in a cracked voice as I stamped on one of the pedals as I had seen Slasher do. The car roared with power; the wheels squealed; it leaped to life, hurtling.

In the wrong direction, backward.

There was an intense crashing and clanging of glass and metal, and the police vanished. I groped for the controls again. One of the fuzz appeared ahead, raising his weapon, but jumped for his life as I found the right combination and the car roared at him. The road was clear, and I was on my way.

With the police in hot pursuit. Before I reached the corner, the other car started up and tore forward. Colored lights began rotating on top of it, and its siren wailed after. I drove with one hand and fumbled with my own controls – spraying liquid on the windscreen, then seeing it wiped away by moving arms, hearing loud music, warming my feet with a hot blast of air – until I also had a screaming siren and, perhaps, a flashing light. We tore down the wide road in this manner, and I felt that this was not the way to escape. The police knew their city and their vehicles and could radio ahead to cut me off. As soon as I realized this, I pulled at the wheel and turned into the next street. Since I was going a bit faster than I should, the tires screeched and the car bounced up onto the sidewalk and caromed off a building before shuddering back into the roadway. My pursuers dropped behind with this maneuver, not willing to make the turn in this same drastic manner, but were still after me when I barreled around the next corner. With these two right-angle turns I had succeeded in reversing my course and was now headed back toward the scene of the crime.

Which may sound like madness but was really the safest thing to do. In a few moments, siren wailing and lights going, I was safe in the middle of a pack of screaming, flashing blue and white vehicles. It was lovely. They were turning and backing and getting in one another's way, and I did what I could to increase the confusion. It was quite interesting with much cursing and the shaking of fists from windows, and I would have stayed longer if reason had not prevailed. When the excitement reached its merriest, I worked my way out and slid my vehicle around the corner. I was not followed. At a more reasonable pace, siren silenced and lights lowered, I trundled along the street looking for a haven. I could never escape in the police car, and I had no intention of doing so; what I needed was a rathole to crawl into.

A luxurious one; I do not believe in doing things halfway. Not very much farther on I saw my goal, ablaze with lights and signs, glittering with ornament, a hotel of the plus and luxury class almost a stone's throw from the site of the crime. The last place where I would be looked for. I hoped. Certain chances have to be taken always. At the next turning I parked the car, stripped off the uniform, put a bundle of bills in my pocket, then trundled back toward the hotel with my two bags. When the car was found, they would probably think I had changed vehicles, an obvious ploy, and the area of search would widen.

'Hey, you,' I called out to the uniformed functionary who stood proudly before the entrance. 'Carry these bags.'

My tone was insulting, my manners rude, and he should have ignored me had I not spoken in another language and pressed a large denomination banknote into his hand. A quick glimpse of this produced smiles and a false obsequiousness as he grabbed for my bags, shuffling after me as I entered the lobby.

Glowing wood paneling, soft rugs, discreet lighting, lovely women in low-cut dresses accompanied by elderly men with low-hung bellies; this was the right place. There were a number of raised eyebrows at my rough clothing as I strode across to the reception desk. The individual behind looked coldly down a long patrician nose, and I could see the ice already starting to form. I thawed it with a wad of money on the counter before him.

'You have the pleasure of meetin' a rich but eccentric millionaire,' I told him. 'This is for you.' The bills vanished even as I offered them. 'I have just come back from the boonies, and I want the best room you got.'

'Something *might* be arranged, but only the Emperor Suite is available and that costs . . .'

'Don't bodder me with money. Take this loot and let me know when you want more.'

'Yes, well, perhaps something can be arranged. If you would be so kind as to sign your name here. . . .'

'What's *your* name?'

'Me? Why, it's Roscoe Amberdexter.'

'Ain't that a coincidence – that's my name, too, but you can call me sir. Must be a very common name around here. So you sign for me since we both got the same name.' I beckoned, and he leaned forward, and I spoke in a hoarse whisper. 'I don't want no one to know I am here. Everyone's after my loot. Send up the manager if he wants more information.' What he would get would be money, which I was sure would do just as well.

Buoyed on a wave of greenbacks, the rest was clear sailing.

I was ushered to my quarters, and I bestowed largess on my two bag carriers for being so smart they didn't drop them. They opened and shut things and showed me all the controls, and I had one of them call room service for much food and drink, and they left in the best of humors, pockets bulging. I put the bag of money in the closet and opened the smaller case.

And froze.

The indicator needle on the time energy detector had moved and was pointing steadily toward the window and the world outside.

## SEVEN

My hands wanted to shake, but I would not let them as I took out the detector and placed it gently on the floor. The field strength was 117.56, and I made a rapid note of this. Then I dropped and sighted along the needle at the exact spot under the window where it pointed. Running over quickly, I marked a big X on this spot, then rushed back to check it. As I took the second sight, the needle began to drift, and the meter dropped to zero.

But I had them! Whoever they were, they were operating out of this era. They had used their time apparatus once, and they were sure to use it again. When they did, I would be waiting for them. For the first time since I had been whipped back to this crude barbarian world I was warmed by a small spark of hope. Up until now I had been operating by reflex, just staying alive and learning to make my way in this strange place, and all of the time keeping my thoughts away from the future that would not exist unless I could bring it into being. And that was just what I was going to do.

After a hearty dinner and a snowfall of fluttering banknotes I went to sleep. Not for long though, a two-hour zonk pill put me under in the deepest possible sleep, with almost constant dreaming, and I awoke feeling much more human. There were a number of interesting bottles in the bar in the next room, some of them rather palatable, and I sat down with a filled glass in front of a glass-eyed instrument called a TV. As I had guessed, my accent in the local language left a lot to be desired, and I wanted to listen to someone who spoke a better form of it.

This was not easy to find. To begin with, it was hard to tell which were the educational channels and which were there for entertainment. I found what appeared to be a morality play in historical form where all the men wore wide-brimmed hats and rode on horses. But the total vocabulary used could not have been more than 100 words, and most of the characters were killed by shooting before I could discover what it was all about. Guns seemed to play an important role in most of the dramas I watched, though this was varied with sadism and assorted kinds of mayhem. All this violence and hurtling from one place to another in various conveyances did not leave the people much time for intersexual activity; a brief kiss was the only manifestation of affection or libido that I saw. Most of the dramas were also difficult to follow since they kept being interrupted by brief playlets and illustrated lectures about the purchase of various consumer goods. By dawn I had had enough of this and my speech had improved only microscopically, so I kicked in the glass picture tube as fitting comment and went to wash myself in a pink room filled with museum pieces out of the history of plumbing.

As soon as the shops opened in the morning, I had a number of hotel employees at work with a great deal of money and my purchases soon poured in. New clothes to fit my high station, with expensive luggage to carry it in. Plus a number of maps, a carefully made gadget called a magnetic compass, and a book on the principles of navigation. It was simplicity itself to determine the exact direction that the detector had pointed and to transfer this to a local map and to get a fairly accurate measurement of the distance in the measurement units called miles to the source of the time energy field. A long black line on the map gave me my direction, a slash across it to show distance – and I had my target. The two lines crossed at what appeared to be a major center of population, in fact, the largest one on this map.

It was called, quaintly, New York City. There was no indication where Old York City was, and it did not matter. I knew where I had to go.

Leaving the hotel was more like a royal abdication than a simple parting, and there were many glad cries for me to hurry back. As well there might be. A hired car whirled me out to the airport, and ready hands rushed my luggage to the proper exit. Where a rude shock was awaiting me since I had completely forgotten about the bank robbery. Others had not.

'Open up da bags,' a grim-looking defender of law and order said.

'Of course,' I said, very cheerily. I noticed that all of the passengers were being subjected to this same search. 'Might I ask what you are looking for?'

'Money. Bank robbery,' he muttered, poking through my possessions.

'I'm afraid I never carry large sums,' I said, holding the bag with my massed banknotes tight to my chest.

'These are OK. Let's see that one.'

'Not in public if you please, officer. I am a high-placed government official, and these papers are top secret.' I quoted this word for word from the TV.

'In the room,' he said, pointing. I was almost sorry I had kicked the thing in since it had been so educational.

In the room he looked shocked when I opened a sleepgas grenade rather than the bag, and he slumped nicely. There was a large metal locker against the wall filled with the numerous forms and papers so dear to the bureaucratic mind, and by rearranging them, I managed to make room for my snoring companion. The longer he remained undiscovered, the better. Unless there were unforeseen delays I would be in New York City before he regained consciousness – a process that would have to be a natural one since there would be no known antidote for my gas.

When I left the room, another of the uniformed officials was glowering at me, so I turned and called back through the still open door. 'Thank you for your kind aid, no trouble at all, I assure you, no trouble at all.' I closed the door and smiled at him as I passed. He raised a reluctant fingertip to the visor of his cap and turned away to grab at the luggage of an elderly passenger. I went on with my bag, not too surprised to notice the finest of pricklings of sweat upon my brow.

The flight was brief, uninteresting, noisy, and rather too

bumpy, in a great fixed-wing craft that appeared to be powered by jets burning a liquid fuel. Though the smell of this fuel was everywhere, and familiar, I could not bring myself to believe that they were burning irreplaceable hydrocarbons. I had a moment of expectation when we disembarked, but there did not seem to be any alarm. Reaching the center of the city from the outlying airport was a painful ordeal of hurtling vehicles, shouts, noise of all kinds, and it was with a feeling of great relief that I finally fell through the door of a cool hotel room. But once reason was restored by the quiet, plus a couple of belts of the distilled organ destroyer I was becoming attached to, I was more than ready for the next step.

Which would be what? Reconnoiter or attack? Sweet reason dictated a careful stalk of the time energy source to determine what I was up against; who and what. I had half settled on this course and was berating myself mildly for even considering attack before the force of logic clanked through to its last link. I turned and pointed at myself in the mirror.

'You are a dum-dum.' I shook a disgusted finger at myself. 'What the cabdriver called the other cabdriver. A joick and woise.'

There was only one advantage that I had – and that was surprise. Any bit of reconnoitering might tip my hand, and the time warriors would know that they were under investigation, perhaps attack. Since they had launched the time war, they were surely prepared for possible retaliation. But how can guards stay alert for weeks and months, possibly years? Once they knew I was around, at this time and place, all sorts of extra precautions would be taken. To prevent this, I had to hit and hit hard – even though I had no idea whom I was hitting.

'Does it make a difference?' I asked, snapping open a grenade case. 'It might be nice to satisfy my curiosity and find out who has attacked the Corps – and why? But is it relevant or important? The answer is no.' I glared across a small atomic fusion bomb at my red-eyed mirrored image and shook my head. 'No, and no again. They must be destroyed, period. Now. Quickly.'

There was no other course open to me, so calmly and surely I fitted about my body the most potent weapons of destruction ever devised by millennia of weapons research, always a favorite of mankind. Normally I am no believer in the kill-or-be-killed school of thought; affairs are usually not that black and white. They were now, and I felt not the slightest guilt over my decision. This was undeclared war against all mankind of the future – or why else had the Special Corps been the first target of attack? Someone, some group, wanted control of *everything*, probably the most selfish and insane plan ever conceived, and it did not really matter who or what they were. Death for them, before they killed everything of value.

When I left the hotel, I was a walking bomb, an army of destruction. The black box of the time energy detector was in the attaché case I carried, the indicators visible through holes I had cut in the lid. Somewhere out there was the enemy, and when he moved, I would be waiting.

It was a short wait. There was an unseen burst of time energy unleashed, close by if the action of the needle was any indication, and I was on the trail. Direction and distance, I worked out the vector as I plunged ahead, almost ignorant of the people and vehicles around me, but slowing and becoming more careful after a close miss by a lumbering truck.

Now a wide thoroughfare with green in the center of it, tall buildings of a uniformly depressing design, great slabs of metal and glass looming up in the polluted air. One very much like the other. Which one did I want?

The needle swung again, quivering with the intensity of its reaction, turning as I walked, the meter rising to a distance reading right at the top of its scale.

There. In that building, the copper and black one.

In I went, prepared for anything.

Anything that is except what happened next.

They were locking the doors behind me, lining up and

blocking them even as they did so. *Everyone*. The visitors to the building, the elevator starters – even the man behind the cigar counter. Running, pressing forward, coming toward me with the cold light of hatred in their eyes.

I had been discovered; they must have detected *my* detector; they knew who I was. They were attacking first.

# EIGHT

It was a nightmare come alive. At some time in our lives we are all touched by incipient paranoia and feel that everyone is against us. Now I was faced with the reality. For a single instant this basic fear possessed me; then I shrugged it off and tried to win.

But that slight hesitation had been enough. What I should have done was shoot, kill, fire, destroy, just as I had planned. But I had not planned to face all these people in this manner; therefore, I could not win. Of course, I did some damage, gas and bombs, a bit of violence, but it wasn't enough. More and more hands tore at my clothing, and there was no end to them. Nor were they gentle about it, coming at me with the same raw hatred I felt for them, opposite sides of the coin, both seeing destruction in the other. I was pursued and run down, and unconsciousness was almost a blessing when it dropped.

Not that I was allowed this peace for long. Pain and a sharp smell burning in my nostrils drew me back to face unpleasant reality. A man, a large, tall man, standing and facing me, his features blurred by my unfocused eyes. It seemed that many hands held me, squeezing tight and shaking me. Something moist was pulled across my face clearing away whatever had obscured my vision, and I could see. See him as he saw me.

Twice as tall as a normal man, so much bigger than me that I had to lean back to look up at him towering there. His skin a suffused red, his eyes angled and dark, many of his teeth pointed when he opened his mouth.

'When are you from?' he asked, his voice a harsh drum, speaking the language we used in the Corps. I must have reacted to that because he smiled, with victory but not with warmth.

'The Special Corps, it had to be. The one flare of energy before darkness. How many of you came? Where are the others?'

'They . . . will find you,' I managed to say. A very minor success for my side weighed against the victories of the other. As yet they did not know that I was alone, and I would stay alive until they discovered it. Which would not be long. I had been stripped efficiently, all my devices removed. My defenses gone. They would backtrack me to the hotel and find out soon enough that there was no more to fear.

'Who are you?' I asked, words my only weapon. He did not answer but instead raised both fists in a victorious gesture. The words came automatically to my lips. 'You're mad.'

'Of course,' he shouted exultantly and the hands holding me pulled and swayed at the same time. 'That is our condition, and though they killed us once for it, they will not kill us again. This time we will be victorious because we will destroy our enemies even before they are born, doom to nonlife oblivion the ones who did it.'

I remembered something Coypu had said about this Earth being destroyed in the far past. Had it been done to stop these people? Was it being undone now? His screamed words cut off the thought.

'Take him. Torture him most profoundly for my pleasure and to weaken his will. Then suck all the knowledge from his brain. Everything must be discovered, everything.'

As the hands tore me from the room, I knew what I had to do. Wait. Get away from this man, away from the crowds, to the specialized skills of the torturers, to some needed privacy. The opportunity came as technicians in a white laboratory beat at the people who held me and dragged me from them. They were as brutal to one another as they had been to me, a hierarchy of hatred. They must be mad as he had said. What perversion of human history had brought these people upon the scene? There was no way to imagine.

Again I waited. Calm in the knowledge that I had only a

single opportunity and I should not throw it away. The door was closed. I was pressed back against a table, and my ankles were secured to it. There were five men in the room with me. Two had their backs turned, attention on their instruments; the others were pushing me down. I moved my jaw forward and bit down as hard as I could upon the last tooth.

This was my final weapon, the ultimate weapon, one that I had never used before. I normally did not even carry it, considering the normal life-and-death dustups not worth this price of winning. The present situation was different. When I bit, the artificial tooth cracked and the drops of bitter liquid it contained ran down my throat.

As the pain hit, it was obliterated, engulfed even as it began by the nerve-deadening drug that enabled me to withstand the onslaught of the other ingredients. They were a devil's brew that the Corps' medics had worked out at my suggestion, that had only been tested before in smaller quantities on test animals. Here were all the stimulants ever discovered, including the new class of synergators, the complex chemicals that enabled the human body to perform the incredible feats of hysterical strength that had been long known but impossible to duplicate.

Time speeded up, and the men hovering above me moved slowly. Seeing this, I waited those fractions of a second more for the drugs to take complete effect before reaching out my hands. Though each of the heavyset men had his full weight on one of my arms, it did not matter. There was no feeling of weight or even effort as I lifted them each clear of the floor at the same time and drove their skulls together before hurling them bodily at the third man at the foot of the table. All of them impacted, rolled, fell, their faces twisted in strange contortions of pain and fear. I sat up even as they dropped and seized the solid metal bands that bound my ankles and tore them free. It appeared to be the easiest and most obvious thing to do. This seemed to cause some damage to my fingers, but I was aware of it only as a passing comment and of no real importance. There were two more men in the room who were still turning toward me as though the destruction of the other three had only taken a few moments. Which it surely had. Seeing them still unprepared, one with a weapon half-raised, I threw myself at them, sparing a fist or a clutching hand for each, striking them down and hurling them toward the others into the writhing bundle of twisting bodies. They were five to my one, and I could afford to show them not even the slightest mercy even had I cared to. I struck, with my feet now since my hands were not so good, until there was no more motion in the heap, and only then could I permit the cold thoughts of logic to penetrate the hot berserker rage.

Next? Escape. My own clothes were rags, and I tore them from me in strips. My torturers were dressed in white garments, and I took the time to open all the unfamiliar fastenings and dress myself in the least soiled of their clothing. There was a ragged wound in my forehead, which I covered with a neat dressing – there would be other bandages here after the battle in the entrance – then put wrappings about my hands. I was not interrupted, it could not have taken long, and when I was done, I left the room and went hurriedly back down the hallway, retracing the course over which I had been so recently dragged. There was a buzz like a disturbed hive in the building, and everyone I passed seemed too preoccupied to notice me, even the people milling about in the anteroom where my weapons had been spread out on a large table to be examined. If it had been a time for smiling, I would have smiled.

Gently, without disturbing anyone, I reached over and actuated a rack of gas bombs, holding my breath as I groped for the nose filters. It is a fast gas, and even those who had seen what I had done had no time for warnings before they fell. The air was hazy with the concentration of the gas when I picked up a gausspistol and threw open the great door to the next room.

'*You!*' he called out, his massive red body standing even as the gas felled the others around him. He swayed and reached

55

for me, fighting the gas that should have dropped him instantly, until I slammed the pistol into the side of his head until he stopped. Yet his eyes, murderous with hatred, were on me all the time as I bound him in the chair. Only when the door was sealed behind me did I take the time to look him in the face again and see that he was still conscious.

'What kind of man are you?' The words were on my lips, unasked. 'Who are you?'

'I am He who will rule forever, the mind that never dies. Release me.'

There was such a power in his words that I felt myself drawn closer, swaying despite myself, the roundness of his eyes growing before me. I was hazy, the effects of my own drugs wearing off perhaps, and I shook my head and blinked rapidly. But another part of me was still alert, still unimpressed by great power, great evil.

'A long rule, but not a comfortable one.' I smiled. 'Unless you do something about that bad case of sunburn.'

It could not have been better spoken. This monster was utterly humorless and must have been used to nothing except slavish obedience. Just once he howled, a speechless animal sound, and then there was speech enough, a torrent of babbled insanity that washed around me as I made preparations to end the time war.

Mad? Of course he was, but with some kind of organized madness that perpetuated and grew and infected those around him. The body was artificial. I could see the scars and grafts now, and he spoke to me about it. A fabricated body, a transplanted, stolen body, a metal-framed monstrosity that told me all too much about the manner of mind that would choose to live in a case like this.

There were others like him, he was the best, he was alone – it was hard to make sense of everything, but I remembered what I could for future reference. And all the time I was taking off the ventilating grille and dusting my powders into the air system and making preparations to throw a large monkey wrench into this satanic mill.

He and his followers had been destroyed once in the fullness of time. He had told me that. In some unknown manner they had planned a second chance at the mastery of the universe – but they were not to have it. I, Slippery Jim diGriz, single-minded freebooter of no fixed address had been called upon for many big tasks before, and I had always delivered. Now I was asked to save the world, and if I must, I must.

'They could not have picked a better man,' I said proudly as I looked in at the great workings of a time laboratory neatly peppered with sprawled bodies. The great green coiled spring of a time-helix glowed at me, and I smiled back.

'Bombs in the works and you for a ride,' I called out happily as I made just those preparations. 'Wipe out the machinery and leave the nuts here for the local authorities, though perhaps Big Red deserves a special treatment.'

He certainly did, and I wondered what I was waiting for. I was waiting to do it in the heat of passion, I imagine, no cold killer I even of the coldest of killers. Though I would have to be this time. I steeled myself to this realization, thumbed the selector on the gausspistol to explosive charges, and turned to the other room.

Opportunity presented itself far more quickly than I had imagined. A great red form was on top of me, striking out, hitting me. I rolled with the blow, across the room to the wall, twisting and bringing up the gun.

He was moving fast, tripping a switch and hurling himself at the end of the time-helix.

Bullets move fast, too, and mine hissed out of the gausspistol and into his body, exploding there.

And then he was gone. Pulled into time, forward or backward I did not know because the machinery was glowing and melting even as I ran. Would he be dead when he arrived at his destination? He had to be. Those were explosive charges.

Some of the drugs were beginning to wear off, and rattling fingers of pain and fatigue were already beginning to scratch at the edge of my awareness. It was time to go. Get my equipment first, then get out. To the hotel and then to a hospital.

A little rest cure while they patched me up would give me the time to consider what to do next. The technology of this era might be advanced enough for the construction of a time-helix, and I still had the professor's memory locked in that black box. I would probably need a lot more money, but there were always ways of getting that.

I exited with an unhealthy stagger.

# NINE

I carried an attaché case filled with the usual things: grenades, gas bombs, explosives, nose filters, a gun or two – just the normal tools of the trade. My back was straight, my shoulders square, and I entered the paymaster's office in a most martial manner. If only to do the uniform justice, a spanking-new gold-striped and beribboned uniform of a commander in the United States Navy.

'Good morning,' I snapped briskly, closing the door behind me and locking it at the same time, swiftly and silently, with the tool concealed in my hand.

'Yes, sir.'

The grizzled chief petty officer behind the desk spoke politely enough, but it was obvious that his attention was really upon his work, the papers that piled neatly upon his desk, and strange officers just had to wait their turn. Just as sergeants do in all armies, the chiefs run the navies. Sailors hurried about on naval financial matters, and through a doorway opposite I had a view of the gape-mouthed gray form of a government issue safe. Lovely. I put my case on the chief's desk and snapped it open.

'I read about it in the newspaper,' I said. 'How the military always rounds its figures upwards to the next million or billion dollars when asking for appropriations. I admire that.'

'Aye, aye, sir,' the chief muttered, his fingers punishing the comptometer keys, uninterested either in my reading ability or in any comments from the press.

'I thought you would be interested. But that gave me the idea. Share the wealth. With such liberality there should be plenty to spare for me. That is why I am going to shoot you, Chief.'

Well, that got his attention. I waited until the eye widen-

59

ing and jaw gaping reached their maximum, then pulled the trigger on the long-barreled pistol. It went *shoof* and thudded in my hand, and the chief grunted and slipped from sight behind the desk. All of this had taken but a moment, and the others in the office were just becoming aware that something was wrong when I turned and picked them off one by one. Stepping over the litter of bodies, I poked my head into the inner office and called out.

'Hoo-hoo, Captain, I see you.'

He turned from the safe, growling some nautical oath, and caught the needle in the side of his neck. He folded as quickly as the others. My drug is potent, swift-acting, and soporific. Already snores were rising from the room behind me. The payroll was there, stacks of crisp bills arranged neatly in a nest of trays. I snapped open my folding suitcase and was reaching for the first bundle of green goodness when the glass crashed out of the window and the gun hammered bullets in my direction.

Only I wasn't there. If they had fired through the glass, I would have been thoroughly punctured by the lead slugs the people of this time favored, but they had not. Breaking the glass before firing gave me that fraction of a second to take action, action that my well-tuned and always-suspicious reflexes were constantly waiting for. I was over and back in a tumbling roll, minibombs from my sleeve holdout dropping into my fingers even before I hit the floor. Both flash and smoke. They thudded and flared, and the air was instantly opaque. I sent more after the first, and the firing stopped. I wriggled along the floor like a snake and, with the bulk of the safe between myself and the window, began stuffing the bag full of money, working by touch. Just because I was discovered, trapped, and in mortal danger was no reason to leave the loot. If I was going to all this trouble, I ought to at least be paid for it.

Dragging both bags behind me, I crawled toward the outer office and was about to go through the doorway when the loudhailer blared outside.

'We know you're in there. Come out and surrender or we'll gun you down. The building is surrounded – you don't have a chance.'

The smoke thinned out near the door, and standing in the darkness, I could see through the windows that the voice had been speaking the truth. There were trucks out there, presumably loaded with hard-eyed well-armed SP's. As well as jeeps with large-caliber machine guns mounted in their rears. Quite a reception committee.

'You'll never take me alive, you rats!' I shouted, sowing smoke and flare bombs in all directions, as well as a larger explosive grenade that took out part of the rear wall. Under cover of all this excitement I crawled over to the sleeping chief and peeled off his jacket by touch. A lad of long service, he had more stripes than a tiger and hash marks up to his elbows. I threw my jacket aside and donned his, then traded hats as well. The people outside seemed to have set an elaborate trap, which meant they knew more about me than I cared to have them know. But this knowledge could be turned against them by a swift change in rank. I flipped about a few more bombs, put my gun into my pocket, picked up both bags, and unlocked and flung the front door open.

'Don't shoot!' I called out in a hoarse voice as I stumbled out into the fresh air and stood in the open doorway, a perfect target. 'Don't shoot – he's got a gun in my back. I'm a hostage!' I tried to look terrified, which required little effort when I saw the small army facing me.

After this I staggered forward a half step and looked over my shoulder, letting everyone get a good view of me. Attempting to ignore the feeling that I had a bull's-eye painted on my chest with the big black spot right over my heart.

No one fired.

I stretched the moment a bit further – then dived off the steps and rolled to one side.

'Shoot! Get him! I'm clear!'

It was most spectacular. All the guns let go at once and blew the door from the frame and the glass from the windows, and the front of the building became as perforated as a colander.

'Aim high!' I called out, crawling for the protection of the nearest jeep. 'All our guys are on the floor.'

They shot high and vigorously and began to separate the top of the building from the bottom. I crept past the jeep and an officer came over to me and collapsed as I broke a sleep-gas capsule under his nose.

'The lieutenant's hit,' I cried as I shoved him and the bags into the back of the jeep. 'Get him out of here.'

The driver was very obliging and did as ordered, barely giving me time to get in myself. Before we had gone five meters, the gunner was sleeping next to the lieutenant, and as soon as the driver shifted into high gear, he dozed as well. It was tricky getting him out of the seat and getting myself into it while bouncing along at a good clip, but I managed it. Then I stood on the gas pedal.

It did not take them long to catch on. In fact, the first of the jeeps was after me even as I was stuffing the driver in back with the others. This barrier of bodies was a blessing because no more guns were going off. But they certainly were in hot pursuit. I did a sharp turn around a building and sent a platoon of boots jumping for cover, then took a fast look at the pursuers. My! Twenty, thirty vehicles of all kinds tore along after me. Cars, jeeps, trucks, even a motorcycle or two, passing one another, horns and sirens going, having a wonderful time. Jim diGriz, benefactor of mankind. Wherever I go, happiness follows. I turned into a large hangar and rushed between rows of parked helicopters. Mechanics dived aside in a cloud of flying tools as I skittered between the machines in a tight turn and back toward the open front of the hangar. As I emerged on one side, my followers were rushing in at the other. Very exciting.

Helicopters – why not? This was Bream Field, the self-proclaimed helicopter capital of the world. If they could fix the things, they could fly them. By now the entire naval station would be locked tight and surrounded. I had to find another way out. Off to one side the green glass form of the tower loomed up, and I headed in that direction. The flight line was before me, and a fat-bellied helicopter stood there, motor rumbling and blades swishing in slow circles. I squealed the jeep to a stop below the gaping door. When I stood up to throw my bags through it, a heavy boot kicked out at my head.

They had been alerted by radio, of course – as probably had everyone else in a hundred-mile radius. It was annoying. I had to duck under the blow, grab the boot, and wrestle with its owner while my horde of faithful followers roared up behind me. The boot owner knew entirely too much about this kind of fighting, so I cheated and shortened the match by shooting him in the leg with one of my needles. Then I threw the money in, hurled some sleepgas grenades after it, and finally myself.

Not wanting to disturb the pilot, who was snoring at the controls, I slipped into the copilot's seat and bugged my eyes at the dials and knobs. There were certainly enough of them for such a primitive device. By trial and error I managed to find the ones that I wanted, but by this time I was surrounded by a solid ring of vehicles, and a crowd of white-hatted club-and-gun-bearing SP's were fighting to be first into the copter. The sleepgas dropped them, even the ones wearing gas masks, and I waited until I had a full load, then pulled the throttle full on.

There have been better takeoffs, but as an instructor once told me, anything that gets you airborne is satisfactory. The machine shuddered and shimmied and wallowed about. I saw men diving for safety below and felt the crunch of the wheels against the top of a truck. Then we were up and sagging away in a slow turn. Toward the ocean and the south. It was not chance alone that had led me to this particular military establishment when my funds ran low. Bream Field is situated in the lower corner of California with the Pacific Ocean on one side and Mexico on the other. Which is as far south and as far west as you can go and stay in the

United States. I no longer wished to stay in the United States. Not with what looked like all the Navy and Marine helicopters in the country rumbling up after me. I'm sure the fighter planes were on the way. But Mexico is a sovereign nation, a different country, and the pursuit could not follow me there. I hoped. At least it would pose some problems. And before the problems had been solved, I would be long gone.

As the white beaches and blue water flew by beneath me, I worked on a simple escape plan. And familiarized myself with the controls. After a bit of trial and error and a few sickening lurches, I found the automatic pilot. A nice device that could be set to hover or to follow a course. Just what I needed. The mere sight of it provided my plan, complete and clear. Below me the border rushed up, then the bullring and the pink, lavender, and yellow houses of the Mexican beach resort. They swept by quickly enough, and the grim coast-line of Baja California instantly began. Black teeth of rocks in the foam, sand and sharp gorges cutting down to the sea, gray mesquite, dusty cactus. An occasional house or camp-site. Dead ahead a rocky peninsula jutted out into the ocean, and I pulled the machine up over it and down on the other side. The rest of the copters were only seconds behind me.

Seconds were all I needed. I set the controls to *hover* and climbed down among the sleeping defenders of the law. The ocean was about ten meters below, the great spinning rotors sending up clouds of spray from it. I threw both my bags out into the water and had turned to inject the pilot in the neck even before they had hit. He was stirring and blinking – the sleepgas antidote is almost instantaneous – as I set the robot pilot for forward flight and dived for the open door.

It was a close-run thing. The copter was moving forward at full blast as I tumbled into the air. It wasn't much of a dive, but I did manage to get my feet down so they hit first. I went under, swallowed some water, coughed, swam up, and banged my head on one of the floating bags. The water was far colder than I had thought it would be, and I was shivering and a cramp was beginning in my left leg. The bag gave me some support so that, kicking and floundering, I splashed over and grabbed the other one. Just as I did this, there was a mighty roar from overhead as the rumbling crowd of helicopters hurtled past like avenging angels. I'm sure that none of them were looking down at the water; all eyes were fixed upon the single copter rushing away ahead of them to the south. Even as I looked, this machine began to bob and turned off in a slow arc. A delta-wing jet appeared suddenly, diving past it and up and around. I had a little time but not very much. And there was absolutely no place to hide on the exposed rock of the peninsula or the bare sand of the shore.

Improvise, I told myself as I paddled and puffed toward the shore. They don't call you Slippery Jim for nothing. Slip out of this one. The cramp took over, and all I felt like doing was slipping under the water. Then there was firm sand under my feet, and I staggered, gasping, up onto the beach.

I had to hide without being hidden. Camouflage, one of mother nature's original tricks. The angry copters were still buzzing about on the horizon as I began to dig furiously at the sand with my bare hands.

'Stop!' I ordered myself and sat up, swaying. 'Use your brains, not your muscles, lesson number one.'

Of course. I slipped an explosive grenade into my hand, triggered it and dropped it into the shallow hole, then dived aside. It whoomphed satisfactorily and sent up a spray of sand. And left a tidy crater that was just the right size for the two bags. I hurled them into it and began to undress frantically, throwing my clothes after the bags. The copters must have been chatting with each other; they were turning and starting back down the beach.

Just by chance, vanity had goaded me this morning into putting on purple underwear which could easily pass for swimming attire from a distance. I stripped down to these shorts and kicked sand into the hole, covering everything.

By the time the first copter swished by overhead I was

lying facedown and sunning myself, just another swimmer on a beach. They went by overhead in a line, making a sweep. I sat up and looked at them as anyone would with all this going on. Then they were past, bobbing up over the rocky spine and gone, their motors rumbling out of hearing.

But not for long, that was certain. What should I do? Nothing. Just stay pat and think innocent. I had elected my role, and now I had to play it out.

They didn't take much time. Whoever was in charge ordered a sweep in line abreast covering the ocean, beach, and hills. Now they were slower, searching every inch of the way, undoubtedly with high-powered glasses. Time for another swim. I shivered when the spray curled around my ankles and knew I was turning blue as the water crept ever upward. A wave broke over my head, and I was swimming with a stately dog paddle.

The copters were back, and one hovered over me, sending up clouds of spray. I shook my fist up at it and shouted realistic curses into the sound of its engine. Someone was leaning out of the open doorway, calling to me, but I was not listening. After a certain amount of fist shaking I submerged and swam underwater, trying to make my one uncramped leg do the work of two. The copter was swinging away after the others as I painfully made my way ashore again and sprawled on the sand so the wind and sun could dry me.

Now how did I get out of here?

# TEN

As soon as the copters were out of sight, I dug like a mole and unearthed my clothing and the bags, rushing them up the beach above the high-water mark. Another bomb and another interment, only this time I put on my trousers and shoes – and made sure some of my equipment went into the pockets. A few quick cuts transformed the long-sleeved uniform shirt into a short-sleeved sport shirt. As this clothing began to dry, it lost all resemblance to any part of a military dress, which was all for the best. Before leaving, I scuffed and dragged the sand to obliterate my digging and took careful triangulations of some large inland peaks so I could find the spot again. Then I headed for the coast road that passed a few hundred meters away.

My luck held. I had no sooner climbed over into the northbound lane when a beetlelike open machine with high wheels came rushing toward me. I raised my thumb in the universal gesture and was answered by a squealing of brakes. I saw now that there were powered surfboards sticking out of the back and there were two tanned young men in the front, their garments even more disarrayed than mine. A fashion, I knew, so perhaps they took me for one of their own.

'Man, you look wet,' one commented as I climbed into the back.

'Man, I was high and took a watery trip.'

'Gotta try that some time,' the driver answered, and the machine hurled itself down the road.

Less than a minute later two hulking black sedans with flashing lights and howling sirens tore down the road in the opposite direction. The large letters 'POLICIA' were painted on their side, and it took very little linguistic knowledge to translate that. My new friends, refusing the offer of refreshment, let me off in downtown Tijuana, then raced away. I

67

sat at an outside table with a large tequila, lime, and salt and realized that I had just escaped from a carefully planned trap.

And a trap it was. That was obvious now that I had the time to stop and think about it. All those jeeps and trucks had not appeared out of thin air, and it is doubtful if that amount of firepower could have been organized so quickly even if an alarm had gone off. I went back over my motions, step by step, and was absolutely sure that I had actuated no alarms.

So how had they known what was going to happen?

They knew because some time-hopper had read the newspapers after the event, then had jumped back in time to give the warning. I had been half expecting this to happen – but that did not mean I had to enjoy it. I licked the salt from the base of my thumb, downed the bulk of the tequila, and bit hard into the lime. The combination tasted marvelous as it burned a course of acid destruction down my throat.

*He* was alive. I had wiped out his organization in this happy year of A.D. 1975, but He had gone on to bigger and worse nastiness in another era. The time war was on again. He and his madmen wanted to control all history and all time, an insane idea that might very well succeed, since they had already wiped out the Special Corps in the future, the one law-abiding organization that might have beaten them. Or rather they had wiped out all of the Corps except me, while I had bounced into the past to wipe out the wiper-outers and in doing so restore the Corps to the probable paths of future history. Big assignment, which I had accomplished 99.9 percent of. It was the vital .1 percent that was still causing trouble, the monster. He who had escaped me at the end of a time-helix even though he had been nicely peppered with exploding slugs from my gun. Probably had armored guts. Next time I would use something stronger. An atomic bomb on his breakfast tray or suchlike.

To work. I *had* hoped that a time-helix could be built to whip me back to the future, or rather ahead to the future;

grammar leaves a certain amount to be desired when it comes to time travel. Back/ahead to the arms of my Angelina and the acclaim of my peers. But not right now since they didn't even exist. Time war is a tricky thing and can be very confusing at times. All of the time might be more accurate. I was very glad that I did not need to know the theory but could just be whipped back and forth by others, like a temporal paddle ball, to do my violent best at whatever assignment was required.

There was little difficulty in obtaining a car and digging up the money early the next morning, although certain plainclothes observers had to be induced to sleep soundly instead of doing their jobs. Smuggling the money back into the United States was even easier, and before noon I was in the offices of Whizzer Electronics, Inc., in San Diego. A large and complete laboratory, a small front office with a not too bright receptionist, and that was it. I had set the place up as best I could, and it was up to Professor Coypu now to take over.

'Do you understand, Prof?' I said, talking to the small black box with his name on it. 'All set up and ready to go.' I shook the box. 'Someday you must tell me how your memories can exist in this recorder or if you don't exist or won't exist in this galaxy because He and his nuts have destroyed the Corps. Better someday you don't tell me. I'm not sure I really want to know.' I held the box up and gave it a scan around the room.

'The finest equipment stolen money can afford. Every up-to-date research tool I could lay my hands on. Stocks of spare parts of all kinds. A supply of raw material. Catalogs from all the electronic, physical, and chemical manufacturers. A large bank balance to draw upon to buy what you need. A pile of signed checks waiting to be filled out. Language lessons neatly taped. Instructions, a history of what has happened, the works. Over to you, Prof, and take it easy with this body. It's the only one we have.'

Before I could change my mind, I lay back on the couch, stuck the contact from the memory box to the back of my neck, and turned on the switch.

'*What's happening?*' Coypu said, slithering into my mind.

'A lot. You're in my brain, Coypu, so don't do anything dangerous.'

'*Most interesting. Yes, your body indeed. Let me move that arm now, stop interfering. In fact, why don't you go away for a bit while I see what is happening?*'

'I'm not so sure that I want to.'

'*Well, you must. Here, I'll push.*'

'No!' I shouted, not that it did any good. A formless blackness pressed down on me, and I spiraled out of sight into a greater darkness below, pushed away by Coypu's electronically magnified memories. . . .

```
time
    goes
        by
            so
                slowly
```

The black box was in my hand; the name 'Coypu' written in rough white letters across its front; my fingers were on a switch that was turned to *off*.

Memory returned, and I staggered mentally and looked around for a chair so I could sit down. Until I discovered that I was already sitting down, so I sat harder.

I had been away, and someone else had been running my body. Now that I was back in charge I could detect faint traces of memories of work, a lot of work, a great period of time, days, perhaps weeks. There were burns and calluses on my fingers and a new scar on the back of my right hand. A tape recorder rustled to life – it must have had a timer to turn it on – and Professor Coypu spoke to me.

'To begin with – do not do this again. Do not allow this recorded memory of my brain into control of your body. Because I can remember everything. I remember that I no longer exist. This brain-in-a-box is all there may ever be of

70

me. If I turn off the switch on it, I cease to be. The switch may never be turned on again. Probably won't. This is suicide, and I am not the suicidal type. Impossibly hard to touch the switch. I think I can do it now. I know what is at stake. Something a lot bigger than the pseudolife of this taped brain. So I will do my best to turn the switch. I doubt if I could do it a second time. As I said, don't do this again. Be warned.'

'I'm warned, I'm warned,' I muttered, turning off the tape while I found myself a drink. Coypu was a good man. The bar was stocked as I had left it, and a treble malt whiskey on the rocks cleared some of the muzziness from my head. I settled down and turned the tape on again.

'To business. Once I began investigating, it became obvious why these temporal criminals chose this particular epoch. A society just bursting into the age of technology, yet the people still with their minds in the Dark Ages. Nationalism, sheer folly; pollution, criminal; intraglobal warfare, madness—'

'Enough lecturing, Coypu, on with the show.'

'—but there is no need to lecture on this subject. Suffice to say that all the materials for a time-helix are available here. And the societal setup is such that a major operation of time tinkering can successfully be concealed. I have constructed a time-helix, and it is coiled and set. I have also built a time tracer and with it have ascertained the temporal position of this creature called He. For reasons best known to him He is now operating out of the fairly recent past of this planet, some one hundred and seventy years ago. I am only guessing now, but I think his entire present operation is a trap. Undoubtedly for you. In some manner I cannot discover he has erected a time block before the year 1805. So you cannot return to an early enough period to catch him as he is building his present establishment. Be wary, he must be working with a large force. I have marked the controls so you can pick any of the five years after 1805 during which they are operating. In a city named London. The choice is yours. Good luck.'

I flicked off the recorder and went after more drink, depressed. Some choice. Pick my own year to get blasted. Nip back into the prescientific past and shoot it out with the minions of He. Even if I won – so what? I would be stranded there for life, stuck in time. A dismal prospect. Yet I had to go. In reality I only had the illusion of choice. He was tracking me down in the year 1975, and the next time he might very well succeed in polishing me off. Far better to carry the fight to him. Rah-rah. I took more drink and reached for the first book on the long shelf.

Coypu had not wasted his time. In addition to wiring up all the hardware, he had collected a neat little library about the years in question, the opening decade of the nineteenth century. London was my destination, and as soon as that was realized, the name of one man became of utmost importance.

Napoleoni Buonaparte. Napoleon the First, Emperor of France and most of Europe and almost the world. His megalomaniacal ambitions rang a bell, for they differed hardly at all from He's own ambition. There was no coincidence here; there had to be a connection. I did not know yet what it was, but I was dismally sure that I would find out quickly enough. In the meantime, I read through all the books on the period until I felt I knew what I had to know. The only bright spot in the whole affair was the fact that England spoke a variety of the same speech as America, so I would not have to put up with any more brain-puncturing language lessons with the memorygram.

Of course, there was the matter of local dress, but there were more than enough illustrations from the period to show me what was needed. In fact a theatrical outfitter in Hollywood supplied me with a complete wardrobe, from knee pants and buttoned jackets to great cloaks and beaver hats. The styles of the time were quite attractive, and I took to them instantly, concealing a number of my devices in their voluminous folds.

Since I would return to the same time in time whatever time I left the present time, I took my time with the arrangements. But eventually, I ran out of excuses. The time had come. My weapons and tools were adjusted and ready; my health was perfect; my reflexes were keen; my morale was low. But what must be done must be done. I appeared in the front office, and the receptionist gaped up at me chewin-gumily from over her confession magazine.

'Miss Kipper, draw up a salary check for four weeks for yourself in lieu of notice.'

'You don't like my work?'

'Your work has been all that I desired. But owing to mismanagement, this firm is now bankrupt. I am going abroad to dodge my creditors.'

'Gee, that's too bad.'

'Thank you for your solicitude. Now if I can sign that check. . . .'

We shook hands, and I ushered her out. The rent was paid for a month ahead, and the landlord was welcome to the equipment left behind. But I had fixed a destruct on the time-helix apparatus that would operate after I had gone. There was enough tinkering with time as it was, and I felt no desire to bring any more players into the game.

It was a labor to jam myself into the space suit with all my clothes on, and in the end, I had to take off both boots and jacket and strap these outside with the rest of my equipment. Heavily laden, I waddled over to the control board and braced myself for a final decision. I knew where I would arrive and, following Coypu's instructions, had set the proper coordinates into the machine days earlier. London was out of the question; if they had any detection apparatus at all, they would spot my arrival. I wanted to arrive far enough away geographically so they would not spot me, but close enough so I would not have to suffer a long journey by the primitive transportation of the time. Everything I had read about it caused me to shudder. So I compromised on the Thames Valley near Oxford. The bulk of the Chilterns would be between me and London and their solid rock would absorb radar, zed rays, or any other detection radiation.

Once I had arrived, I could make my way to London by water, a matter of some one hundred kilometers, rather than by the ghastly roads of the period.

That was where I was arriving – when was another matter. I stared intensely at the neatly numbered dials as though they could tell me something. They were mute. A time barrier set up at 1805, I could not arrive earlier. The year 1805 itself seemed too much of a trap; they would surely be ready, waiting and alert at that time. So I had to arrive later. But not too much later, or they would have accomplished whatever evilness they had in mind. Two years then, not too long for them to work, but enough time so that they might – hopefully – be a little off guard. I took a deep breath and set the dials for 1807. And pressed the actuator. In two minutes the time would cut in full power. With leaden feet I shuffled toward the glowing green coil of the time-helix and touched the barlike end.

As before, there was no sensation, just the glow surrounding me so that the room beyond was hard to see. The two minutes seemed closer to two hours, although my watch told me there were more than fifteen seconds to go to spring-off. This time I closed my eyes, remembering the uneasy sensations of my last time-hop, so I was tense, nervous, and blind when the helix released and hurled me back through time.

Zoink! It was not enjoyable. As the helix unwound, I was whipped into the past while its energy was expended into the future. An interesting concept that did not interest me in the slightest. For some reason this trip churned up my guts more than the last one had, and I was very occupied with convincing myself that whoopsing inside a space suit is a not nice thing. When I had this licked, I realized that the falling sensation was caused by the fact that I *was* falling, so I snapped open my eyes to see that I was in the midst of a pelting rainstorm. And dimly seen, close below, were sodden fields and sharp-looking trees rushing up at me.

After some panicky fumbling with the wrist control for the

grav-chute, I managed to turn it on full, and the harness creaked and groaned at the sudden deceleration. I creaked and groaned, too, as the straps felt as though they were slicing through my flesh to the bone beneath – which they would quickly abrade away. I honestly expected my arms to drop off and my legs to fly by when I crashed down through the small branches of a waiting tree, caromed off a larger branch, and crashed into the ground below. Of course the grav-chute was still working on full lift, and as soon as the grassy slope had broken my fall, I was up and away again, hitting the branch a second lick for luck on the way by and springing up out of the treetop in a great welter of twigs and leaves. Once more I fumbled for the control and tried to do a better job of it. I drifted down, around the tree this time, and dropped like a sodden feather onto the grass and lay there for a bit.

'A wonderful landing, Jim,' I groaned, feeling all over for broken bones. 'You ought to be in the circus.'

I was battered but sound, which fact I realized after a painpill had cleared my head and numbed my nerve endings. Belatedly, I looked around through the lessening rain but could see no one – or any sight of human habitation. Some cows in the adjoining field grazed on, undisturbed by my dramatic appearance. I had arrived.

'To work,' I ordered myself, and began to unburden myself under the shelter of the large tree. The first thing off was the collapsible container I had constructed with great ingenuity. It opened out and assembled into a brassbound leather chest typical of the period. Everything else, including the space suit and grav-chute, fitted into it. By the time I had loaded and locked it the rain had stopped and a frail sun was working hard to get through the clouds. Midafternoon at least, I judged by its height. Time enough to reach shelter by nightfall. But which way? A rutted path through the cow field must lead someplace, so I took that downhill, climbing the drystone fence to reach it. The cows rolled round eyes in my direction but otherwise ignored me. They were large

75

animals, familiar to me only through photographs, and I tried to remember what I had heard about their pugnacity. These beasts apparently did not remember either and did not bother me as I went down the path, chest on shoulder, setting out to face the world.

The path led to a stile which faced onto a country lane. Good enough. I climbed over and was considering which direction to take when a rustic conveyance made its presence known by a great squeaking and a wave of airborne effluvium carried by the breeze. It clattered into sight soon after, a two-wheeled wooden artifact drawn by a singularly bony horse and containing a full load of what I have since determined to be manure, a natural fertilizer much valued for its aid to crops and its ability to produce one of the vital ingredients of gunpowder. The operator of this contrivance was a drab-looking peasant in shapeless clothes who rode on a platform in front. I stepped into the road and raised my hand. He tugged on a series of straps that guided the pulling beast and everything groaned to a stop. He stared down at me, chomping empty gums in memory of long-vanished teeth, then reached up and knuckled his forehead. I had read about this rite, which represented the relationship of the lower class to the upper classes, and knew that my choice of costume had been correct.

'I am going to Oxford, my good man,' I said.

'Ey?' he answered, cupping one grimy hand behind his ear.

'Oxford!' I shouted.

'Aye, Oxford,' he nodded in happy agreement. 'It be that way.' He pointed back over his shoulder.

'I'm going there. Will you take me?'

'I be going that way.' He pointed down the lane.

I took a golden sovereign out of my wallet, purchased from an old coin dealer, more money in one lump than he had probably seen in his entire lifetime, and held it up. His eyes opened wide and his gums snapped nicely.

'I be going to Oxford.'

The less said about this ride, the better. While the un-sprung dungmobile tortured the sitting part of my anatomy, my nose was assaulted by its cargo. But we were at least going in the correct direction. My chauffeur cackled and mumbled incomprehensibly to himself, wild with glee at his golden windfall, urging the ancient nag to its tottering top speed. The sun broke through as we came out of the trees, and ahead were the gray towers of the university, pale against the darker slate gray of the clouds, a very attractive sight indeed. While I was admiring it, the cart stopped.

'Oxford,' the driver said, pointing a grubby finger. 'Magdalen Bridge.'

I climbed down and rubbed my sore hams, looking at the gentle arch of the bridge across the small river. There was a thud next to me as my chest hit the ground. I started to pro-test, but my transportation had already wheeled about and was starting back down the road. Since I was no more desirous of entering the city in the cart than he was of taking me, I didn't protest. But he might at least have said some-thing. Like good-bye. It didn't really matter. I shouldered the chest and strode forward, pretending I did not see the blue-uniformed soldier standing by the shack at the end of the bridge. Holding a great long gunpowder weapon of some sort that terminated in what appeared to be a sharp blade. But he saw me well enough and lowered the device so it blocked my way and pushed his dark-bearded face close to mine.

'*Casket vooleyfoo?*' he said, or something like that. Im-possible to understand, a city dialect perhaps since I had no trouble understanding the rustic who had brought me here.

'Would you mind repeating that?' I asked in the friendliest of manners.

'*Koshown onglay,*' he growled and whipped the wooden lower end of his weapon up to catch me in the midriff.

This was not very nice of him, and I showed my distaste by stepping to one side so the blow missed and returned the favor by planting my knee in his midriff instead. He bent in

77

the middle, so I chopped him in the back of the neck when that target presented itself. Since he was unconscious, I seized his weapon so it would not be actuated when it dropped.

All this had happened in the shortest of times, and I was aware of the wide-eyed stares of the passing citizenry. As well as the ferocious glare of another soldier in the door of the ramshackle building, who was raising his own weapon toward me. This was certainly not the way to make a quiet entrance into the city, but now that I had started I had to finish.

With the thought the deed. I dived forward, which enabled me to put down my chest while I avoided the weapon at the same time. There was an explosion, and a tongue of flame shot by my head. Then the butt of my own weapon came up and caught my latest opponent under the chin, and he went back and down with me right behind him. If there were others inside, it would be best to tackle them in the enclosed space.

There certainly were other soldiers, a goodly number of them, and after taking care of the nearest ones with a little dirty infighting, I triggered a sleepgas grenade to silence the rest. I had to do this – but I didn't like it. Keeping a wary eye on the door, I quickly mussed the clothing and kicked the ribs of the men who had succumbed to the gas in order to suggest that they had been felled by violence of some kind.

Now how did I get out of this? Quickly was the best idea since the citizenry would have spread the alarm by now. Yet when I reached the doorway, I saw that the passersby had drawn close and were trying to see what had happened. When I stepped out, they smiled and shouted happily, and one of them called out loudly.

'A cheer for his lordship! Look what he done to the Frenchies!'

Glad cries rang out as I stood there, dazed. Something was very wrong. Then I realized that one fact had been nagging at me ever since I had my first look at the colleges. The flag, flying proudly from atop the nearest tower. Where were the crossed crosses of England?

This was the tricolor of France.

# ELEVEN

While I was trying to figure this one out, a man in plain brown leather clothes pushed through the cheering crowd and shouted them into silence.

'Get home, the lot of you, before the frogs come and kill you all. And don't say a word about this or you'll be hanging from the town gate.'

Looks of quick fear replaced the elation, and they began to move at once, all except two men who pushed past to pick up the weapons strewn about inside. The sleepgas had dispersed, so I let them pass. The first man touched two fingers to his cap as he came up to me.

'That was well done, sir, but you'll have to move out quick because someone will have heard that shot.'

'Where shall I go? I've never been to Oxford before in my life.'

He looked me up and down quickly, in the same way I was sizing him up, and came to a decision.

'You'll come with us.'

It was a close-run thing because I heard the tread of heavy marching boots on the bridge even as we nipped down a side lane burdened with the guns. But these men were locals and knew all the turnings and bypaths, and we were never in any danger that I could see. We ran and walked in silence for the better part of an hour before we reached a large barn that was apparently our destination. I followed the others in and put my chest on the floor. When I straightened up, the two men who had been carrying the guns took me by the arms while the man in leather held what appeared to be an exceedingly sharp knife to my throat.

'Who are you?' he asked.

'My name is Brown, John Brown. From America. And what is your name?'

'Brewster.' Then, without changing the level tone of his voice: 'Can you give me reason why we should not kill you for the spy you are?'

I smiled calmly to show him how foolish the thought was. Inside, I was not calm at all. Spy, why not? What could I say? Think fast, Jim, because a knife kills just as thoroughly as an A-bomb. What did I know? French soldiers were occupying Oxford. Which meant that they must have invaded England successfully and occupied all or part of it. There was resistance to this invasion, the people holding me proved that, so I took my clue from this fact and tried to improvise.

'I am here on a secret mission.' Always good. The knife still pressed against my throat. 'America, as you know, sides with your cause. . . .'

'America helps the Frenchies; your Benjamin Franklin has said so.'

'Yes, of course, Mr. Franklin has a great responsibility. France is too strong to fight now, so we side with her. On the surface. But there are men like me who come to bring you aid.'

'Prove it?'

'How can I? Papers can be forged, they would be death to carry in any case, and you wouldn't believe them. But I have something that speaks the truth, and I was on my way to London to deliver it, to certain people there.'

'Who?' Had the knife moved away the slightest amount?

'I will not tell you. But there are men like you all over England, who wish to throw off the tyrant's yoke. We have contacted some of the groups, and I am delivering the evidence I spoke of.'

'What is it?'

'Gold.'

That stopped them all right, and I felt the grip on my arms lessen ever the slightest. I pressed the advantage.

'You have never seen me before and will probably never see me again. But I can give you the help you need to buy weapons, bribe soldiers, help those imprisoned. Why do you think I assaulted those soldiers in public today?' I asked with sudden inspiration.

'Tell us,' Brewster said.

'To meet you.' I looked slowly around at their surprised faces. 'There are loyal Englishmen in every part of this land who hate the invaders, who will fight to hurl them from these green shores. But how can they be contacted and helped? I have just shown you one way – and have provided you with these arms. I will now give you gold to carry on the struggle. As I trust you, you must trust me. If you wish, you will have enough gold to slip away from here and live your lives out happily in some kinder part of the world. But I don't think you will. You risked your lives for those weapons. You will do what you know is right. I will give you the gold and then go away. We will never meet again. We must go on trust. I trust you. . . .' I let my voice dwindle away, allowing them to finish the sentence for themselves.

'Sounds good to me, Brewster,' one of the men said.

'Me too,' said the other. 'Let's take the gold.'

'*I'll* take the gold if there's any to be taken,' Brewster said, lowering the knife but still uncertain. 'It could all be a lie.'

'It could be,' I said quickly, before he started punching holes in my flimsy story. 'But it isn't – nor does it matter. You'll see that I'm well away tonight, and we will never meet again.'

'The gold,' my guard said.

'Let's see it,' Brewster said reluctantly. I had bluffed it through. After this he couldn't go back.

I opened the chest with utmost care while a gun was kept pressed to my kidney. I had the gold; that was the only part of my story that was true. It was divided into a number of small leather bags and intended to finance this operation. That is just what it was doing now. I took one out and solemnly handed it over to Brewster.

He shook some of the glittering granules into his hand, and they all stared at it. I pushed.

'How do I get to London?' I asked. 'By river?'

'Sentries on every lock of the Thames,' Brewster said, still looking at the golden gravel upon his palm. 'You wouldn't get as far as Abingdon. Horse, the only way. Back roads.'

'I don't know the back roads. I'll need two horses and someone to guide me. I can pay, as you know.'

'Luke here will take you,' he said, finally looking up. 'Used to be a drayman. But only to the walls; you'll have to get by the Frenchies yourself.'

'That will be fine.' So London was occupied. And what about the rest of England?

Brewster went out to take care of the horses, and Guy produced some coarse bread and cheese, as well as some ale, which was more welcome. We talked, or rather they talked and I listened, occasionally putting in a word but afraid of asking any questions that might prove my almost total ignorance. But a picture finally developed. England was completely occupied and pacified, had been for some years; the exact number was not made clear, although fighting was still going on in Scotland. There were dark memories of the invasion, great cannon that did terrible damage, the Channel fleet destroyed in a single battle. I could detect the cloven hoof of He behind a lot of it. History had been rewritten.

Yet this particular past was not the past of the future I had just come from. My head started to ache just thinking about it. Did this world exist in a loop of time, separate from the mainstream of history? Or was it an alternate world? Professor Coypu would know, but I did not think he would enjoy being plucked out of his memory tape again just to answer my questions. I would have to work it out without him. Think, Jim, put the old brain-box into gear. You take pride in what you call your intelligence, so apply it to something besides crookery for a change. There must be some form of logic here. Statement A, in the future this past did not exist. B, it sure existed now. But C might indicate that my presence here would destroy this past, even the memory of this past. I had no idea how this might be accomplished, but it was such a warm and cheering thought that I grabbed onto it. Jim diGriz history changer, world shaker. It made a pleasant image, and I treasured it as I dozed off on the hay – and woke up not too long afterward scratching at the invading insect life that was after my hot body.

The horses did not arrive until after dark, and we agreed that it would be best to leave at dawn. I managed to get some bug spray out of my chest to kill off my attackers, so I enjoyed a relatively peaceful night before the ride in the morning.

The ride! We were three days en route, and before we reached London, even my saddle sores had saddle sores. My primitive companion actually seemed to enjoy the trip, treating it as an outing of sorts, chatting about the country we passed through and getting falling down drunk each evening at the inns where we stopped. We had crossed the Thames above Henley and made a long loop to the south, staying away from all sizable centers of population. When we reached the Thames again at Southwark, there was London Bridge before us and the roofs and spires of London beyond. A little hard to see because of the high wall that stretched along the opposite riverbank. The wall had a crisp, clean look to it, far different from the smoke-stained gray of the rest of the city – and a sudden thought struck me.

'That wall, it's new, isn't it?' I said.

'Aye, finished two years back. Many died there, women and children, everyone driven like slaves by Bony to put it up. Right around the city it goes. No reason for it, just that he's mad.'

There was a reason for it, and ego-flattering as it was, I still didn't like it. That wall was built for me, to keep me out. 'We must find a quiet inn,' I said.

'The George, right down here.' He smacked his mouth loudly. 'Good ale, too, the best.'

'You enjoy it. I want something right on the river, within sight of that bridge there.'

'Knows just the place, the Boar and Bustard on Pickle

Herring Street, right at the foot of Vine Lane. Fine ale there.'

The foulest brew was fine by Luke as long as it contained alcohol. But the Boar and Bustard suited my needs perfectly. A disreputable establishment with a cracked signboard above the door depicting an improbable-looking swine and an even more impossible-looking bird squaring off at each other. There was a rickety dock to the rear where thirsty boatmen could tie up – and a room I could have that looked out on the river. As soon as I had arranged for the stabling of my horse and argued over the price of the room, I bolted the door and unpacked the electronic telescope. This produced a clear, large, detailed, depressing picture of the city across the river.

It was surrounded by that wall, ten meters high of solid brick and stone – undoubtedly bristling with detection apparatus of all kinds. If I tried to go under or over it, I would be spotted. Forget the wall. The only entrance I could see from this vantage point was at the other end of London Bridge, and I studied this carefully. Traffic moved slowly across the bridge because everything and everyone was carefully searched before they were allowed to enter. French soldiers probed and investigated everything. And one by one the people were led through a doorway into a building inside the wall. As far as I could tell, they all emerged – but would I? What happened inside that building? I had to find out, and the ale room below was just the place.

Everyone loves a free spender, and I was all of that. The one-eyed landlord muttered and snaffled to himself and managed to find a drinkable bottle of claret in his cellar which I kept for myself. The locals were more than happy to consume blackjack after blackjack of ale. These containers were made of leather covered with tar which added a certain novelty to the flavor, but the customers did not seem to mind. My best informant was a bristle-bearded drover named Quinch. He was one of the men who moved the cattle from the pens to the knackers' yard where he also assisted the butchers in their bloody tasks. His sensibilities, as one might suspect, were not of the highest, but his capacity for drink was, and when he drank, he talked, and I hung on every word. He entered and left London every day, and bit by bit, through the spate of profanity and abuse, I put together what I hoped was an accurate picture of the entrance procedures.

There was a search; that much I could see from my window. At times a close search, at other times superficial. But there was one part of the routine that never varied.

Every person entering the city had to put his hand into a hole in the wall of the guardhouse. That was all, just put it in. Not touch anything at all, just in up to the elbow and out.

Over this I brooded, sipping my wine and ignoring the roars of masculine cheer around me. What could they detect from this? Fingerprints perhaps, but I always wore false fingerprint covers as a matter of routine and I had changed these three times since the last operation. Temperature? Skin alkalinity? Pulse or blood pressure? Could these residents of, what to me was, the dim past differ in some bodily composition? It was not unreasonable to expect some changes over a period of more than 30,000 years. I had to find out the present norms.

This was done easily enough. I constructed a detector that could record all these factors and hung it inside my clothing. The pickup was disguised as a ring that I wore on my right hand. The next evening I shook hands with everyone I could, finished my wine, and retired to my chamber. The recordings were precise, accurate to $\pm 0.006$ percent and very revealing. Of the fact that my personal readings fell well inside all the normal variations.

'You are not thinking, Jim,' I accused myself in the warped mirror. 'There *has* to be a reason for that hole in the wall. And the reason is a detection instrument of some kind. Now what does it detect?' I turned away from the accusing stare. 'Come, come, don't evade the question. If you cannot answer it that way, turn it on its head. What is it possible to detect?'

This was more like it. I pulled out a piece of paper and began to list all the things that can be observed and measured, going right down the frequencies. Light, heat, radio waves, etc., then off into vibration and noise, radar reflections, anything and everything, not attempting to apply the things detected to the human body. Not yet. I did this after I had made the list as complete as possible. When I had covered the paper, I shook hands with myself triumphantly and reread it for human applications.

Nothing. I was depressed again. I threw it away – then grabbed it back. Something, what was it, something relating to something I had heard about Earth. What? Where. *There!* Destroyed by atomic bombs Coypu had said.

Radioactivity. The atomic age was still in the future, the only radioactivity in this world was natural background radiation. This did not take long to check.

Me, creature of the future, denison of a galaxy full of harnessed radiation. My body was twice as radioactive as the background count in the room, twice as radioactive as the hot bodies of my friends in the bar when I slipped down to check them out.

Now that I knew what to guard against I could find a way to circumvent it. The old brain turned over, and soon I had a plan, and well before dawn I was ready to attack. All the devices secreted about my person were of plastic, undetectable by a metal detector if they had one working. The items that were made of metal were all in a plastic tube less than a meter long and no thicker than my finger, which I coiled up in one pocket. In the darkest hour before the dawn I slipped out and stalked the damp streets looking for my prey.

And found him soon enough, a French sentry guarding one of the entrances to the nearby docks. A quick scuffle, a bit of gas, a limp figure, a dark passageway. Within two minutes I emerged at the opposite end wearing his uniform with his gun on my shoulder carried in the correct French manner. With my tube of devices down its barrel. Let them find *that* metal with a detector. My timing was precise, and when, at the first light, the straggling members of the night guard returned to London, I was marching in the last row.

I would enter, undetected, in the ranks of the enemy. A foolproof scheme. They wouldn't examine their own soldiers.

More fool I. As we marched through the gate at the far end of the bridge I saw an interesting thing that I could not see with my telescope from my window.

As each soldier marched around the corner of the guardhouse he stopped for a moment, under the cold eyes of a sergeant, and thrust his hand into a dark opening in the wall.

# TWELVE

'Mayerd!' I said as I tripped over the uneven footing on the bridge. I did not know what it meant, but it was the most common word the French soldiers used and seemed to fit the occasion. With this I stumbled into the soldier next to me, and my musket caught him a painful blow on the side of the head. He yelped with pain and pushed me away. I staggered backward, hit my legs against the low railing – and fell over into the river.

Very neatly done. The current was swift, and I went beneath the surface and clamped the musket between my knees so I wouldn't lose it. After that I surfaced just once, splashing at the water and screaming wordlessly. The soldiers on the bridge milled about, shouting and pointing, and when I was sure I had made the desired impression, I let my wet clothes and the weight of the gun pull me under again. The oxygen mask was in an inside pocket, and it took only seconds to work it out and pull the strap over my head. Then I cleared the water from it by exhaling strongly and breathed in pure oxygen. After that it was just a matter of a slow, easy swim across the river. The tide was on the ebb so the current would carry me well downstream from the bridge before I landed. So I had escaped detection, lived to regather my forces and fight again, and was totally depressed by my complete failure to get past the wall. I swam in the murky twilight and tried to think of another plan, but it was not exactly the best place for cogitation. Nor was the water that warm. Thoughts of a roaring fire in my room and a mug of hot rum drove me on for what seemed an exceedingly long time. Eventually I saw a dark form in the water ahead which resolved into the hull of a small ship tied up at a dock; I could see the pilings beyond. I stopped under the keel and worked my tube of instruments out of the musket and also took everything out of my coat. The gun stuffed into the jacket sleeve made a good weight, and both vanished toward the river bottom. After some deep breathing I took off the oxygen mask and stowed that away as well, then surfaced as quietly as I could next to the ship.

To look up at the coattails and patched trousers of a French soldier sitting on the rail above me. He was industriously involved polishing the blue-black barrel of a singularly deadly-looking cannon that projected next to him. It was far more efficient looking than any of the nineteenth-century weapons I had seen, which was undoubtedly caused by the fact that it did not belong to this period at all. Out of more than casual interest I had made a study of weapons available in the era I had recently left, so I recognized this as a 75-millimeter recoilless cannon. An ideal weapon to mount on a light wooden ship, since it could be fired without jarring the vessel to pieces. It could also accurately blow any other wooden ship out of the water long before the other's muzzle-loading cannon were within range. Not to mention destroying armies in the field. A few hundred of these weapons brought back through time could alter history. And they had. The soldier above turned and spat into the river, and I sank beneath the surface again and vanished among the pilings.

There were boat steps farther downriver out of sight of the French ship, and I surfaced there; no one was in sight. Dripping, cold, depressed, I climbed out of the water and hurried toward the dark mouth of the lane between the buildings. There was someone standing there, and I scuttled by – but then decided to stop.

Because he put the muzzle of a great ugly pistol into my side.

'Walk ahead of me,' he said. 'I will take you to a comfortable place where you can get dry clothing.'

Only he did not say clothing, it sounded more like cloth-eeng. My captor very positively had a French accent.

All I could do was follow instructions, prodded on by the primitive hand cannon. Primitive or not, it could still blow a nice hole in me. At the far end of the lane a coach had been pulled up, blocking the lane completely, the door gaping open in unappreciated welcome.

'Get in,' my captor said, 'I am right behind you. I saw that unfortunate soldier fall from the bridge and drown and I thought to myself, what if he had been on the surface? What if he were a good swimmer and could cross the river, where would he land when moved along by the current? A neat mathematical problem which I solved, and *voilà!* there you were coming out of the water.'

The door slammed, the coach started forward, and we were alone. I fell forward, dropped, turned, lunged, grabbed out for the pistol – and seized it by the butt because my captor now had it by the barrel and was holding it out to me.

'By all means you hold the gun, Mr. Brown, if it pleases you; it is no longer needed.' He smiled as I gaped and scowled and leveled the pistol at him. 'It seemed the simplest way to convince you to join me in the carriage. I have been watching you for some days now and am convinced that you do not like the French invaders.'

'But – you are French?'

'But of course! A follower of the late king, a refugee now from the land of my birth. I learned to hate this pipsqueak Corsican while people here were still laughing at him. But no one laughs any longer, and we are united in one cause. But, please, let me introduce myself. The Count d'Hesion, but you may call me Charles since titles are now a thing of the past.'

'Pleased to meet you, Charley.' We shook on it. 'Just call me John.'

The coach clattered and groaned to a stop then, before this interesting conversation could be carried any further. We were in the courtyard of a large house and, still carrying the pistol, I followed the count inside. I was still suspicious, but there seemed little to be suspicious of. The servants were all ancient and tottered about muttering French to one another. Knees creaking, one aged retainer poured a bath for me and helped me to strip, completely ignoring the fact that I still held the pistol while he soaped my back. Warm clothes were provided, and good boots, and when I was alone, I transferred my armory and devices to my new clothing. The count was waiting in the library when I came down, sipping from a crystal glass filled with interesting drink, a brimming container of the same close by him. I handed him the pistol, and he handed me a glass of the beverage in return. It glided down my throat like warm music and sent a cloud of delicate vapor into my nostrils the like of which I had never inhaled before.

'Forty years old, from my own estate, which as you can tell instantly is in the Cognac.'

I sipped again and looked at him. Nobody's fool. Tall and thin with graying hair, a wide forehead, lean, almost ascetic features.

'Why did you bring me here?' I asked.

'So we could join forces. I am a student of natural philosophy, and I see much that is unnatural. The armies of Napoleon have weapons that were made nowhere in Europe. Some say they come from far Cathay, but I think not. These weapons are served by men who speak very bad French, strange and evil men. There is talk of even stranger and more evil men at the Corsican's elbow. Unusual things are happening in this world. I have been watching for other unusual things and am on the lookout for strangers. Strangers who are not English, such as yourself. Tell me – how can a man swim across a river under water?'

'By using a machine.' There was no point in silence; the count knew very well what he was asking. With those dark cannon out there there was no point in secrecy about the nature of the enemy. His eyes widened as I said this, and he finished his drink.

'I thought so. And I think you know more about these strange men and their weapons. They are not of the world as we know it, are they? You have knowledge of them, and you are here to fight them?'

'They are from a place of evil and madness, and they have brought their crimes with them. And I am fighting them. I cannot tell you everything about them because I don't know the entire story myself. But I am here to destroy them and everything they have done.'

'I was sure of it! We must join forces, and I will give you whatever help I can.'

'You can begin by teaching me French. I have to get into London, and it appears I will need to speak it.'

'But – is there time?'

'An hour or two will do. Another machine.'

'I am beginning to understand. But I am not sure that I like all these machines.'

'Machines cannot be liked or disliked; they are immune to emotion. We can use them or misuse them, so the problem of machines is a human problem like all others.'

'I bow to your wisdom; you are, of course, right. When do we begin?'

I returned to the Boar and Bustard for my things, then moved into a room in the count's house. A head-splitting evening with the memorygram – headache is a mild word for the side effects of using this memory-cramming machine – taught me conversational French, and to the count's pleasure, we now conversed in that language.

'And the next step?' he asked. We had dined, and dined well indeed, and were now back to the cognac.

'I need to take a closer look at one of those pseudo Frenchmen who seem to be running things. Do they ever appear alone on this side of the river or, if not alone, in small groups?'

'They do, but their movements follow no set pattern. Therefore I shall obtain the most recent information.' He rang the silver bell that stood next to the decanter. 'Would you like one of these individuals rendered unconscious or dead and brought to you?'

'You are too kind,' I said, holding out my glass so that the servant who had soundlessly appeared could refill it. 'I'll handle that end of the business myself. Just point him out and I'll take over from there.'

The count issued instructions; the servant slipped away; I worked on my drink.

'It will not take long,' the count said. 'And when you have the information, do you have a plan of action?'

'Roughly. I must enter London. Find He, the top demon in this particular corner of hell, then kill him, I imagine. And demolish certain machinery.'

'The upstart Corsican – you will remove him, too?'

'Only if he gets in the way. I am no common murderer and find it difficult to kill at any time. But my actions should change the entire operation. The new weapons will no longer be supplied and will soon run out of ammunition. In fact, the interlopers may vanish altogether.'

The count raised one eyebrow but was kind enough not to comment.

'The situation is complex; in fact, I do not really understand it myself. It has to do with the nature of time, about which I know very little. But it seems that this past, the time we are living in now, does not exist in the future. The history books to come tell us that Napoleon was beaten, his empire wiped out, that Britain was never invaded.'

'It should only be!'

'It *may* be – if I can get to He. But if history is changed again, brought back to what it should have been, this entire world, as we know it now, may vanish.'

'A certain risk must be taken in all hazardous enterprises.' The count remained cool and composed, moving one hand in a slight gesture of dismissal as he talked. An admirable man. 'If this world disappears, it must mean that a happier one will come into existence?'

'That's roughly it.'

'Then we must press on. In that better world some other I will be returning to my estates, my family will live again, there will be flowers in the spring and happiness in the land. Giving up this life here will mean little; it is a miserable existence. Though I would prefer that knowledge of this possibility stay locked in this room. I am not sure that all our assistants will accept such a philosophical viewpoint.'

'I agree heartily. I wish it could be some other way.'

'Do not concern yourself, my dear friend. We will talk of it no longer.'

We didn't. We discussed art and viniculture and the hazards inherent in the manufacture of distilled beverages. Time moved quickly – as did the count's men – and even before we started on a second decanter, he was called out to receive a report.

'Admirable,' he said upon his return, rubbing his hands together with pleasure. 'A small party of the men we seek are even now disporting themselves in a knocking shop in Mermaid Court. There are guards about, but I presume that offers no barrier to your operation?'

'None,' I said, rising. 'If you will be kind enough to provide some transportation and a guide, I promise to return within the hour.'

This was done as asked, and I performed as promised. A morose individual with a shaved head and badly scarred face took me in the carriage and pointed out the correct establishment. I entered the building next to it, an office of some kind, now shuttered and locked with a monstrous piece of hardware most difficult to open. Not that the lock mechanisms were beyond me – never! – but they were so big that my lockpick couldn't reach the tumblers! My knife did, though, and I went through and up to the roof and crossed over to the roof of the next building, where I attached the end of my spider web to the most solid of the collection of chimneys. The strand of the web was a fine, almost invisible and practically unbreakable strand made up of a single long-chain molecule. It ran slowly off the reel that was fastened by a harness to my chest, and I dropped down toward the dark windows below. Dark to others. But the dual beams of ultraviolet light from the projectors on my UV sensitive goggles turned all light as day for me wherever I looked. I entered the window silently, caught my man with his pants down, rendered him and his companion unconscious with a dose of gas, and had him dozing in my arms and back up to the roof as quickly as the fiercely whirring spider web reel could lift us. Minutes later my prize was snoring on a table in the count's cellar while I spread out my equipment. The count looked on with interest.

'You wish to obtain information from this species of pig? I do not normally condone torture, but this seems to be an occasion for hot pokers and sharp blades. The crimes these creatures have committed! It is said the New World aborigines can flay a person completely without killing him.'

'Sounds jolly, but there will be no need.' I lined up the instruments and hooked up the contacts. 'Machines again. I shall keep him unconscious and walk through his mind with spiked boots, even a worse torture in many ways. He will tell us what we need to know without ever knowing he has spoken. Afterward he is yours.'

'Thank you, no.' The count raised disgusted hands. 'Whenever one of them is killed, the civilians suffer from many reprisals and killings. We will knock this one about a bit, rob him of clothing and everything, then dump him in an alley. It will resemble a crime of robbery, nothing else.'

'The best idea yet. Now I begin.'

It was like swimming in a sewer, going through that mind. Insanity is one thing, and he was certifiably insane like all of them, but outright evil is inexcusable. There was no problem in exacting information, just in sorting it out. He wanted to speak his own language but finally settled for French and English. I plumbed and picked and probed and eventually discovered all that I needed to know. Jules, my companion of the shaved head, was called in for the pleasurable sport of roughing up the subject and dumping him – stripped of his uniform – while the count and I returned gratefully to the unfinished carafe.

'Their headquarters appears to be in a place called St. Paul's. You know of it?'

'Sacrilege, they halt at nothing! The cathedral, the masterpiece of the great Sir Christopher Wren, it is here on the map.'

'The one named He is there, and apparently all the machinery and instruments as well. But to reach it, I must enter London. There is a good possibility that I might be able to pass the wall in his uniform since his body has the same radioactivity count as mine, a test they use to detect strangers. But there may be passwords, other means of identification, perhaps speaking in their own language. What is needed is a diversion. Do you have anyone with a knowledge of gunnery among your followers?'

'Certainly. René Dupont is a former major of artillery, a most knowledgeable soldier. And he is in London.'

'Just the man. I am sure he will enjoy operating one of those high-powered guns. We shall capture a gun ship before dawn. At first light when the gates are opened the bombardment will start. A certain number of shells through the gate, guardhouse and guard should be disconcerting. Then the boat will be abandoned, and the gunners will escape on foot. This will be the responsibility of your men.'

'It will be a pleasurable task that I shall personally supervise. But where will you be?'

'Marching into the city with the troops, as I tried to once before.'

'Most hazardous! If you are too early, you will be apprehended as you appear or perhaps destroyed in the bombardment. Too late and the gate will be sealed against entry.'

'Therefore we must time things exceedingly well.'

'I will send for the finest chronometers obtainable!'

# THIRTEEN

Major Dupont was a red-faced and gray-haired man with an impressive rotundity of belly. But he was energetic enough and knew his gunnery and was now consumed with a fierce passion to operate the invaders' incredible weapon. The former crew of the gunboat, including the lookouts, slept a deeper sleep than they had planned belowdecks as I worked out the mechanism of the recoilless cannon and explained it to the major. He grasped it instantly and beamed with fierce joy. After his experience with irregular cannon barrels, muzzle-loaded uneven shot, slow-burning powder, and all the rest of the handicaps of his trade, this was a revelation.

'Charge, fuse, and projectile in the same casing, marvelous! And this lever swings open the breach?' he asked.

'Correct. Keep away from these vents when firing since the exhausted gas from the explosion comes out here, canceling the recoil. Use the open sights, the range is so short. I imagine there will be no need to allow for windage at this distance, and there will also be scarcely any projectile drop. The muzzle velocity is much greater than you are used to.'

'Tell me more!' he said, stroking the smooth steel.

Step two. The count would see to it that the ship was moved upstream before dawn and anchored to the embankment below London Bridge. I would see to it that I arrived on the bridge at the agreed-upon time. His nautical chronometer was as big as a cabbage, handmade of brass and steel, and it clacked loudly. But he assured me of its accuracy, and we set it from my atomic watch, as big as my fingernail and accurate to within one second a year. This was the last thing to be done, and as I rose to leave, he put out his hand and I took it.

'We will always be thankful for your aid,' he said. 'There is new hope now among the men, and I share their enthusiasm.'

'It is I who should be thanking you for the help. Considering the fact that my winning might be the worse thing for you.'

He dismissed that thought as unimportant: a very brave man. 'In dying we win as you have explained. A world without these swine is victory enough. Even if we are not there to witness it. Do your duty.'

I did. Trying to forget that the fate of worlds, civilization, whole peoples rested upon my actions. A slip, an accident, and it would be all over for everyone. There could therefore be no accidents. As mountain climbers do not look down and think about the drop below, I put thoughts of failure from my mind and tried to think of a joke to cheer myself up. None came to mind instantly, so I thought instead about putting paid to He and his operation, and this was cheering indeed. I looked at my watch. It was time to leave, so I went quickly without looking back. The streets were deserted, all honest men were at home in bed, and my footsteps echoed from the buildings along the dark street. Behind me the first gray of approaching dawn touched the sky.

London is full of dark alleys that provide ideal sites for lurking, so I lurked craftily within sight of London Bridge and watched as the first soldiers appeared. Some marched in step, some straggled, all looked tired. I was feeling tired myself, so I sucked on a stimtab and kept an eye on my watch. Ideally I should be on the bridge when the firing began, far enough from the gate not to be hit, yet close enough to get through it during the excitement after the barrage. From my vantage point I timed various groups of soldiers crossing the bridge until I had a good estimate. The digits rolled by on my watch, and at the proper moment I took a military brace with my shoulders and stepped out smartly.

'*Lortytort?*' a voice called out – and I realized it was calling to me. I had been so concerned with the time I had stupidly ignored the fact that He's future-fiends would be crossing the bridge as well.

I waved, made an evil grimace, and stepped out smartly.

The man who had called out looked puzzled, then hurried after me. By my uniform he knew I was one of his gang, but one unfamiliar to him. Probably asking me how things were back in the home asylum. I wanted no conversation with him, particularly since I didn't speak his language. I hurried on – painfully aware of him hurrying after me. Then realized I was going too fast and at my present pace I would reach the gate just in time to be blown up.

There was no time to curse my lack of awareness – just a matter of picking what kind of trouble I wanted. Getting blown up was just a little too much to get involved with now. I could see that the gunboat was in position and that figures were on deck. Wonderful. I could almost hear the explosions already. With me in the middle of them. I would have to stop, here, at the appointed spot. I did. Heavy footsteps hammered up behind me and a hand caught at my shoulder, spinning me about.

'*Lortilypu?*' he cried out; then the expression on his face changed, his eyes widening, his mouth opening. '*Blivit!*' he shouted. He recognized me, perhaps from photographs.

'Blivit is the word,' I said and shot him in the neck with the narcotic needle gun I had palmed. But there was another cry of *Blivit!* and one of his teammates pushed through the soldiers, and I had to shoot him, too. This naturally interested everyone nearby, and there were some startled shouts and a certain amount of weapon lifting. I put my back to the bridge parapet and wondered if I would have to shoot the entire French Army.

I did not. The first shell, not too well aimed by the major of horse artillery, hit the bridge not ten meters from where I was standing.

The explosion was considerable, and the air was filled with hurtling pieces of masonry and steel. I dropped as did all the others, some of them permanently, and I took the opportunity to put needles into all the nearest soldiers who had witnessed my earlier shootout.

Back on the boat Dupont was learning to master his weapon

and the next shell struck the city wall. There was much shouting and running about among the men on the bridge and I shouted and milled with the best of them, looking on with pleasure as the next shell whistled cleanly through the gate and blew up the guardhouse inside. Now most of the motion was away from the gate, as well it should be, so I dropped and wormed my way closer on my belly. Shells were now bursting in and around the gate and causing a satisfying amount of destruction. A quick look at my watch informed me that it was almost time for the barrage to lift. The signal would be a shell hitting the wall far from the bridge. After this a few more shots would be fired for effect at targets of opportunity – but no more at the gate.

The shell struck the wall a good hundred meters down-river, blowing a neat hole in it. I jumped to my feet and ran.

What a fine destructive mess. Wreckage and crumbled masonry everywhere, dust and the reek of high explosive in the air. If there had been any survivors here of the bombardment, they had long since left. I scrambled over the rubble, slid down the other side, and nipped around the first corner. The only witnesses to this unstealthy entrance were a couple watching from a doorway, English by their dress, who turned and ran as soon as they saw me. Despite my little tangle on the bridge, the plan had worked perfectly.

The cannon on the river began firing again.

This was not part of any plan, not at all. Something had gone wrong. After the last shots my accomplices were to have retreated to shore and removed themselves to safety. Then two explosions sounded, almost at the same time. The cannon could not fire that fast.

There was another gun shooting.

The street I was on, Upper Thames Street, ran parallel to the wall. I was far enough from the bridge now so my presence would not be associated with the action there – and a ladder climbed up to the top of the wall to an observation platform there. Now empty. Perhaps prudence should have dictated a single-minded continuation of my plans. But I have spent many years not listening to that particular voice, and I was not prepared to start now. One quick look around – no one in sight – and up the ladder. From the top I had a perfect view of the action.

The major was still manning his gun, busily firing away at another gunboat that was coming upriver under full sail. The newcomer, even though handicapped by a moving platform, was more experienced and accurate with his weapon. A shell had already blown a great hole in the stern of my ally's boat, and even as I watched, another hit amidships, and the gun was silent, its barrel in the air and the gunner gone. A figure ran across the deck and dropped into the now-harmless boat. I dug out my electronic telescope and trained it on the deck, knowing what I would see even before I put it to my eye.

It was the count come to the aid of his troops. But even as he jumped aboard, the major rose, blood running down his face, and manned the gun again. It swung about, aiming at the other boat, and hit it squarely with the next shot.

Well done, right at the waterline below the enemy weapon. The gun was silenced, the ship sinking. When I looked back at the major again, I saw that he had retrained his cannon and was firing at the bridge, at the enemy soldiers there. And the count was loading for him. They both were smiling and seemed to be enjoying themselves. The firing continued, faster now, and I let myself back down the ladder.

Neither of them could be blamed; they knew exactly what they were doing. Firing back at last at the enemy they had hated all these years, using a superior and highly destructive weapon. Both would stay there firing until they were cut down. Perhaps they wanted it that way. If this sacrifice were to have any value at all, I had to get on with my own job.

I had studied the count's map well. Along Duck's Foot Lane to Cannon Street and then left. There were people about now, frightened civilians hurrying by, soldiers marching on the double in the opposite direction. No one paid any attention to me at all.

And there, up ahead at the end of the street, the great bulk of the walls and dome rose up, unmistakably St. Paul's.

The end of another road was very near. My final meeting with He.

# FOURTEEN

I was scared. A man is either a liar – or mad – who claims never to have felt fear. I have been touched by it often enough to recognize its smell, but never have I felt the iron hand clamping down as it did now. Ice water in the veins, a hammering in the heart, a rooted feeling in the feet. With a decided effort I grabbed my brain by the throat, no mean feat that, and gave it a good shaking.

Speak, brain, I commanded. Why this sudden case of acute chickenitis? Why the yellow stripe right down the back as far as the heels? Body and brain, we have been in tight spots before, even narrower ones. But we bulled through and came out the other side. Usually victors. What is new here?

The answer came back very quickly. As a rustproof rodent I had penetrated behind the walls of society, doing it on my own and standing or falling on my own. Adventure, rah-rah. But now there was too much riding on the bet, too many people's lives dependent on my actions. Too many! Hopping hafnium, the future survival of the entire galaxy might be at stake. It was almost unbelievable.

'Make it unbelievable,' I muttered, digging in my medikit. If I kept dwelling on what was at stake, I would take no risks, probably take no action. I have never resorted to artificial morale before, but there is a first time for everything. I carried the berserker pills as a sort of amulet; I knew they were there if I ever needed them, therefore I never needed them. Until now. I clicked open the case and brushed the dust off an innocent-looking capsule.

'Get out there and fight, Jim,' I said, then swallowed the thing.

They are outlawed everywhere, and for good reason. Not only because they are habit-forming to a great degree, both physically and psychologically, but for social reasons. Inside the gelatin capsule lies a specific form of madness, a compound that dissolves the conscience and morality of civilized man. Superid takes over. No morals, no conscience – and no fear. Nothing but a great chunk of ego and the sure knowledge of might and right, divine permission to do anything and not to feel concern or fear while doing it. Politicians loaded on berserkerite have toppled regimes and controlled worlds. Athletes have broken all sports records, often destroying themselves or their opponents while accomplishing this. Not nice stuff.

Very nice stuff. I had one fleeting instant of conscience and realization of change as the chemicals took hold of my brain, but it passed even as it began.

'I have come for you, He,' I said, smiling with real joy.

This was power unlimited, the most exhilarating sensation I had ever experienced, a cleansing wind blowing out all the dusty corners of my brain. Do what you want, Jim, what you will, because you are the only power in the world that really counts. How blinded I had been for years. Cramped little moralities, puny affections for others, destructive other-orientated love. How crippled I had been. I love myself because I am God. At last I understood the meaning of God that the old religions were always mumbling about.

I am I, the only power in the entire universe. And He is in that building ahead, thinking with mortal foolishness that he can best me, stop me, even kill me. Now we shall see what happens to idiot plans like that.

A stroll around the premises. A solid enough structure, no apparent guards, undoubtedly loaded with detection apparatus. A subtle or secret approach? Not wise. The only advantage I had was surprise, that and the ability to be absolutely ruthless. I was well armed, a walking engine of death, and no one would stop me. Entry would be simple enough, others were going in and out constantly, all in this same uniform, and there was a buzz and a disturbed whine to this beehive at the present. They did not like the attack on the gate. I must strike now while they were disturbed. All devices at the ready and instantly available, I completed my leisurely circuit of the building and started up the white stone steps at its front.

The cathedral was immense, appearing even larger now with all the pews and religious furniture cleared away. I stalked down the length of the long nave as though I owned it, which I did. Weapons ready at my fingertips. The nave was deserted, and all the activity was concentrated at the far end in the apse where the altar usually stood. This was gone, and in its place was an ornate throne.

In which He was sitting. Arrogant with power, his great red body leaning forward to issue orders to his assistants below. A long table reached across the transept here, littered with maps and papers and surrounded by brilliantly uniformed officers. They appeared to be taking their orders from a man in a simple blue uniform coat. He was very short with a black lick of hair across his forehead. From the description this must be the tyrant Napoleon. Passing on instructions from He as I had expected. I knew I was smiling as I shifted my fingertips closer to my weapons.

A familiar crackling of light caught my attention from the secondary apse off to the right – and my smile broadened. The gleaming machinery of a time-helix was stuffed in there with the technicians bent over their tasks. They would be dead soon, like everyone else here. And I would have temporal transportation out of this barbarian era. I would have to leave a small atomic grenade behind when I went. The end was just about in sight.

No one paid the slightest attention to me as I came up to the table. I would have to use sleepgas first since this would work on them all at the same time. Plenty of time to kill the slaves after I had removed their master.

One concussion grenade, two thermite grenades. I triggered them with my thumb and threw them, one – two – three, in high arcs into He's lap. While they were still in the air I rolled handful after handful of gas grenades down the table under the shocked faces of the officers. The grenades were still hissing and banging as I spun about and used my needle gun – I didn't want to injure the controls! – to shoot down the technicians around the time-helix.

It was all over in a matter of seconds. Quiet descended as the last unconscious body fell. Before turning back, I hurled grenades down the length of the nave so that anyone entering would walk into the gas cloud. Then I looked at He.

Lovely. A roaring pillar of fire with something in its core that might have been a man. The throne burned as well and the column of greasy smoke roiled up toward the great dome above.

'You are beaten, He, beaten,' I shouted leaning forward across the table to get a better look. He would not be surviving this attack.

Napoleon lifted his head from the table and sat up.

'Don't be foolish,' he said.

I wasted no time in thought but tried to kill him. But he was ready and fired before I did with the tubelike weapon concealed in his palm. Fire washed across my face; then it was numb, my body numb, everything, no control. I dropped facedown onto the table. Nor could I feel Napoleon's hands when he rolled me over. He was looking down at me, smiling, roaring with victorious laughter, laughter with more than an echo of madness in it. And he was watching my face as well, my eyes which I could still control, waiting for the widening that meant I understood at last.

'That is right!' he shouted. 'I am He. You have lost. You have burned, destroyed that fine android whose only function was to deceive you into that action. It was a trap for you, everything here, even the existence of this world, this loop in time, has no function other than in being a trap for you. Did you forget so quickly that a body is merely a shell for me, the eternal He? My brain has mastered death and lives on. Now in this imitation of a mad emperor. He never knew what real madness was.

'You have lost – and I have won forever!'

## FIFTEEN

This was a temporary setback. I suppose that normally I would have felt defeated, afraid, angry, suffered under some kind of useless emotion. Now I just waited for the opportunity to kill He again. This was getting very boring; after two tries he was still alive. I resolved that the third would be the final one.

He bent and tore at my clothes, searching me with brutal thoroughness. Ripping my clothing into hanging shreds, pulling off devices that adhered to my skin, taking the knife from my ankle, the gun from my wrist, the tiny grenades from my hair. Within seconds every weapon I could reach was gone. The few weapons and devices left were well out of reach. Very thorough. The search over, he discarded me, flinging my limp body face upward onto the table.

'I have prepared everything for this moment, everything!' He bubbled as he talked, and saliva streaked his chin. I heard the rattle of chains as he picked up my wrists and snapped heavy metal fetters about them. They were joined together by a short length of heavy chain. As the cuffs closed, there was a brief flash of light as the ends welded together, and though I could feel nothing, I saw the instant blistered redness of my skin inside the metal. Not important. Only when this was done did he put a needle into my wrist.

Feeling began to return, first to my hands, great pain in my wrists, and then to my arms. There seemed to be a lot of pain associated with the return of sensation. I ignored this although spasms shook my body uncontrollably. In the end I shook myself off the table, falling heavily and uncontrollably to the floor. He bent and picked me up at once, dragging me across the width of the great cathedral. His strength, even in the disguise of this small body, was tremendous.

In the brief instant I had lain on the floor I had grabbed

something with my fingers. I did not know what it was, other than small and metallic, and it was now clenched tightly in my fist.

There was a solid metal pillar, waist-high, that stood about five meters from the time-helix controls. This too was waiting for me. He held my wrists apart and laid the chain that joined them into a groove in the top of the pillar. There was another flash of light as the chain was welded to the solid metal. He released me, and I swayed but did not fall. Sensation and control were returning to my body, and I mastered it as he went to the controls and made some adjustments. The vast cathedral was silent; we were alone except for the huddled bodies.

'I have won!' he screamed suddenly, doing a little dance step that sent spittle flying from his chin. He pointed to the coiled form of the time-helix and laughed out loud. 'Do you realize that you are now in a loop of time that does not exist, that I called into being to trap you, that will vanish as soon as I leave it?'

'I suspected that. Napoleon lost in our textbooks.'

'He won here. I gave him the weapons and aid to conquer the world. Then I killed him when my new body was ready. This loop in time came into being when I did that, and its existence created a barrier in time that will go down as soon as it ceases to exist. When I leave, this will happen, but not instantly; that would be too easy for you. I want to think of you here, alone, knowing that you have lost and that your future will never exist. There is a time-fixator on this building. It will be here after London and the entire world are gone, perhaps longer than you. You might even die of thirst before it shuts off. Then again you may not. I have won.'

He screamed this last as he turned to the controls again. I opened my fist to see what weapon I had in my palm that might defeat him at this final moment.

It was a small brass cylinder that weighed no more than a few grams. One end had small holes punched in it, and when I turned it over, fine white sand came out. A sander, used for drying the writing ink on papers. I might have wished for a better weapon, but this would have to do.

'I leave,' He said, actuating the mechanism.

'What about the men of yours here?' I asked, needing time to think.

'Mad slaves. They vanish with you, having served my purpose. I have an entire world of them waiting to welcome my return. Soon there will be many worlds; soon it will all be mine.'

There was nothing much I could add to that. He sauntered across the flagstones, a monster in the body of that tiny man, and touched his hand to the glowing end of the time-helix and was instantly engulfed by its cold green flame.

'All mine,' he said, the same green fire glowing in his eyes.

'I don't think so.'

I juggled the sander in my hand, testing its weight, measuring the distance to the controls. I could reach it easily. The settings for the time scale were a bank of keys, not unlike the keys of a musical instrument, and a number of them were depressed now. If I could push one more of them down, the setting would be changed; He would arrive at a different time and place, perhaps not arrive at all. I swung my hand in slow arcs, estimating the distance, the trajectory the little tube must follow to reach the correct place.

He must have seen what I was doing because he began to howl with insane rage, pulling at the time field that neatly held him tight to the end of the helix. Coldly I judged the distance until I was sure I had it right.

'Like this,' I said and tossed the sander in a high arc toward the controls.

It rose up, glinting brightly in a shaft of sunlight from a stained glass window, and arced down.

Striking on the bank of keys, then falling off to rattle to the floor.

He's enraged cries cut off as the time-helix released and He vanished from sight. At the same moment this happened the light changed, dimming to dusk. Outside all the windows there was now just gray. I had seen this before during the time attack on the laboratory that had started everything. London, the world outside, everything, no longer existed. Not in this particular part of time and space. Just the cathedral had existence, held briefly by the time-fixator.

Had He won? I felt the first touch of worry; the effects of the drug must be wearing off. I looked hard, but it was almost impossible to see the indicator dials in the dim light. Had one of them moved just before the helix was actuated? I could not be sure. And it didn't really matter, not to me here. Whether the future was hell or a paradise of peace could not affect me. With the return of emotions I felt a desire to know if my world would ever exist. Would there be a Special Corps and would my Angelina someday be born? I would never know. I tugged sharply at the chains, but of course they held fast.

The end. End of everything. The emotions that were returning were only the blackest and most depressed, but I could not help it. End.

# SIXTEEN

Have you ever been trapped in St. Paul's Cathedral in the year A.D. 1807 with the entire world vanished into non-existence outside, alone and welded to a steel post and soon to vanish yourself? Not many people can answer yes to that question. I can – but can truthfully add that I do not enjoy this singular distinction.

Without much reluctance I am forced to admit that I felt somewhat depressed. I struggled a bit against the metal cuffs that held my wrists, but my heart wasn't really in it. They were too tight and secure, and I knew this kind of helpless thrashing about would be just the sort of thing that He would enjoy with mad passion.

For the first time in my life I felt utter and absolute defeat. It had a darkening and dulling effect on my thoughts – as though I already had one foot in the grave – that removed any idea of struggle and suggested instead that the easiest thing would be to simply give in and await the final curtain. The sensation of defeat was so strong that it blanketed almost all feelings of rebellion against this untimely fate. I should be fighting, thinking of a way out, yet I just didn't want to try. I was more than a little amazed at my submission.

It was while I was engrossed in this navel-examining introspection that the sound began. A distant whine just on the edge of audibility, so weak that I would never have heard it had it not been for the absolute silence of nonexistence wrapped about my cathedral-sized tomb. The sound grew and grew, as annoying as an insect, making me aware of it although I did not wish to be made aware of anything except my sensation of overwhelming defeat. In the end it was quite loud, coming from empty space somewhere high above beneath the dome. I looked up despite my lack of interest just as there was the loud bang of displaced air.

A figure appeared in the darkness above, someone in a space suit. Wearing a grav-chute because he drifted down slowly before me. I was stunned and ready for almost anything when he opened the dark faceplate of his space suit.

Ready for almost anything other than the fact that he was not a he.

'Get rid of that silly chain,' Angelina said. 'You always manage to get into trouble as soon as I leave you alone. You're coming away with me right now, and that is all there is to it.'

There was very little to say even had I been unstunned enough to say it. So I did a fine moronic gaping act and rattled my chains a bit as, light as a falling leaf, she drifted down to the floor. In the end her undoubtedly physical presence jounced my open synapses closed, and I did my best to rise to the occasion.

'Angelina, truly named. You descend from above to save me.'

She opened the faceplate of her space suit wider so she could kiss me through the opening, then took an atomic lance from her belt and began to cut away my chains. 'Now tell me what all this mysterious time-travel nonsense is about. And talk fast, we have only seven minutes; at least that is what Coypu said.'

'What else did he tell you?' I asked, wondering just how much she knew.

'Now don't you start being mysterious with me, Slippery Jim diGriz! I've had enough of that with Coypu.'

I jumped back hastily as she waved the atomic lance under my chin, then beat out the fire that was smoldering on the front of my garments. An angry Angelina can be quite dangerous.

'My love,' I said emotionally, attempting to embrace her while keeping an eye on the lance at the same time. 'I conceal nothing from you, nothing! I know better. It is just that my brain is tied in knots from all this time traveling, and I want to know where your knowledge leaves off before I continue with the complete story.'

'You know perfectly well that I talked to you last on the phone. Big rush, you said, top priority, get over fast you shouted – then rang off. So I did, to Coypu's lab, where everyone was running about and playing with the machinery and too busy to tell me anything. Back in time, they shouted, nothing else. And that horrid Inskipp no better. He said you vanished, just vanished out of his office while he was reading the riot act to you. Apparently he found out about that little bit of money you are putting aside for a rainy decade or two. There was a lot of babble about you saving the world or the galaxy or something, but I couldn't understand a word of it. And all of this went on for a *very* long time, until they could send me back here.'

'Well, I did,' I said modestly. 'Saved you, saved the Corps, saved the whole thing.'

'I was right, you have been drinking.'

'Not in entirely too long a time,' I muttered petulantly. 'If you want to know the truth, you all vanished, poof, just like that. Coypu was the last one to go, so he can tell you about it. The Corps, everyone, they were never born, never existed, except in my memory. . . .'

'My memory is slightly different.'

'It would be. Since through my efforts He's evil plan was foiled. . . .'

'*His* not *he's*. All that drinking has affected your speech.'

'*He* is his name – and I haven't had a drop in hours. Can you possibly listen without interrupting? This story is complicated enough in any case. . . .'

'Complicated and possibly alcoholically inspired.'

I groaned. Then kissed her, longer and warmer this time, a distraction we both enjoyed. This softened her a bit, so I rushed on before she remembered that she was supposed to be angry at me.

'A time attack was launched against the Special Corps, so Professor Coypu whisked me back in time to foil the nefarious scheme. I did all right in 1975, but He got away, went back to whenever he came from, then set up an elaborate trap here in 1807 to trap me. Which he did. But his plans didn't work completely because I managed to change the setting on the time-helix so he was sent to a different time from that he had planned. This must have defeated his time-war plans because you appeared to rescue me.'

'Oh, darling, how wonderful of you. I knew you could save the world if you really tried.'

Mercurial of mood is the word for my Angelina. She kissed me with what can only be described as true passion, and I, clanking my lengths of chain, got my arms around her in happy response when she squawked and straight-armed me, so I reeled back, choking.

'The time!' She looked at her watch and gasped. 'You made me forget. There is less than a minute left. Where is the time-helix?'

'Here!' Hugging my still-painful midriff, I showed her the machine.

'And the controls?'

'These.'

'How ugly. Where is the readout?'

'These dials.'

'This is the setting we must use, down to the thirteenth decimal position Coypu said, most insistent about that.'

I played the keys like a mad pianist and sweated. The dials spun and hesitated, then gyrated wildly.

'Thirty seconds,' Angelina said sweetly, to encourage me. I sweated harder.

'There!' I gasped as she announced ten seconds. I kicked in the timer and threw the master switch. The time-helix glowed greenly at us as we rushed to its protruding end.

'Stay close and hug me as hard as you can,' I said. 'The time field has a surface effect, so we must be close.' She responded with pleasure.

'I only wish I weren't wearing this silly space suit,' she whispered, nibbling my ear. 'It would be so much more fun.'

'It might be, but it might also be a little embarrassing

when we arrived back at the Special Corps in that condition.'

'Don't worry about that, we're not going back yet.'

There was a sudden stab of anxiety just below my sternum. 'What do you mean? Where are we going?'

'I'm sure I wouldn't know. All Coypu said was that the hop would be about 20,000 years into the future, just before this planet is to be destroyed.'

'He and his mad mob again,' I wailed. 'You've just sent us off to tackle an entire planetary insane asylum – where they're all against us!'

Everything froze as the time-helix actuated and I was whipped into time with that pained expression on my face. That expression lasted 20,000 years, which was exactly how I felt.

## SEVENTEEN

Blam! It was like falling into a steam bath – and falling was the right word for it. Hot clouds of vapor rushed past us, and the invisible surface could be ten meters or ten miles below us.

'Switch on your grav-chute,' I shouted. 'Mine's back in the nonexistent nineteenth century.'

Perhaps I shouldn't have shouted because Angelina turned the thing on at full lift and slithered up out of my fond embrace like an oiled eel. I clutched madly and managed to grab one of her feet with both hands – whereupon the boot part of the one-piece space suit promptly came off her foot.

'I wish you wouldn't do that,' she called down to me.

'I agree with you completely,' I answered incoherently through tight-clamped and grating teeth.

The suit stretched and stretched until the leg was twice its normal length and I bobbed up and on down as though I were on the end of a rubber band. I took a quick look, but there was still only fog visible below. Space suit fabric is tough, but it was never designed to take a strain like this. Something had to be done.

'Cut your lift!' I called out, and Angelina responded instantly.

We were in free fall, and as soon as the tension was relieved, the leg fabric contracted and snapped me back up to Angelina's waiting arms.

'Yum,' I said.

She looked down and shrieked and hit the grav-chute power again. This time I wasn't ready and I slipped right down and out of her embrace and was falling toward the solid-looking landscape that had suddenly appeared below.

In the small fraction of a second left to me I did what little I could. Twisting in the air, spreading my arms and legs wide, trying to land square on my back. I had almost succeeded when I hit.

Everything went black, and I was sure I was dead, and darkness overwhelmed my brain as well, and my last thought flashed before me. Not only did I not regret anything I had ever done, but there were a few things I wished I had done more often.

I could not have been unconscious more than a few instants. There was foul-tasting mud in my mouth, and I spluttered it out and rubbed even more of it from my eyes and looked around me. I was floating in a half-liquid sea of mud and water from which large bubbles rose and broke with slow plops. They stank. Sickly-looking reeds and water plants grew on all sides.

'Alive!' I shouted. 'I am alive.' I had struck flat out on the syrupy surface, dividing the blow over the entire back surface of my body. There were some aches and bruises, but nothing seemed to be broken.

'It looks very nasty down there,' Angelina said, hovering a few feet above my head.

'It's just as nasty as it looks so, if you don't mind, I would like to get out of it. Can you sort of drop down so I can grab your ankles, which will permit you to drag me out with a wet sucking sound?'

It was a large wet sucking sound as the decaying quagmire fought to hold onto me, parting only reluctantly with a slobbering sigh. I hung from my love's ankles as we drifted over an apparently endless swamp which vanished in the fog in all directions.

'There, over to the right,' I called out. 'Looks like a channel with running water. I think a wash and brushup are in order.'

'Since I am upwind of you, I couldn't agree more.'

The current was moving slowly, but still moving as I could tell by a tree trunk that drifted by. In the middle of the sluggish stream was a golden sandbar that seemed made for us. I dropped as Angelina came low, and even before she had settled down herself, I was out of the noisome clothes and scrubbing the muck off in the water. When I bobbed up, spluttering, I saw that she had peeled off the sweltering space suit and was combing out her long hair, which happened to be blond at the present moment. Very lovely and I was thinking the most romantic thoughts when fierce fire pierced my gluteus maximus, and I shot straight up out of the water, yiping like a dog whose tail has been caught in the door. As attractive and feminine as she was, Angelina was still Angelina, and the comb vanished to be replaced by a gun, and almost before I touched the sand, she had fired a single well-aimed shot.

While she was applying a bandage to the double row of toothmarks in my derriere, I looked at the fish, half blown apart but still twitching, that had mistaken me for lunch. Its gaping mouth had more teeth than a dental supply house, and there was a definitely evil look in its rapidly clouding eye. Grabbing it by the tail to evade its still-gnashing jaws, I threw it far out into the water. This started a tremendous flurry of action under the surface, and from the size of some of the things that leaped out and smacked back down I saw that I had been attacked by one of the smaller ones.

'Twenty thousand years has done no good at all to this planet,' I said.

'Finish rinsing off that mud, and I'll stand guard. Then we'll have some lunch.' Ever the practical woman.

While I scrubbed, she shot up the pescatorial predators who came after me, including one large fish with fat flanks and rudimentary legs that waddled out of the water in an attempt to have me for lunch. We had it instead; the flanks concealed some fine thick filets that roasted well over a low-set heat projector. Angelina had had the foresight to bring a flask of my favorite wine, which made the meal a memorable one. After which I sighed, eructated, and wiped my lips with satisfaction.

'You have saved my life more than once in the last twenty thousand years,' I said. 'So I no longer am brimful of anger for being whisked to this steambath world rather than back to the Corps. But can you at least tell me what happened and what Coypu told you?'

'He tends to mumble a good deal, but I got the gist of it. He has been working on his time tracker or whatever he calls it and followed your jumps through time, as well as someone he referred to as the enemy, the one you call He. The enemy did something with time, created a probability loop that lasted about five years, then terminated. Then He left this collapsing loop – and you didn't. That's why Coypu sent me back, to the minutes just before it ended, to bring you out. He gave me the setting for the time-helix that would enable us to follow He to this time. I asked him what we were supposed to do here but he kept muttering, "Paradox, paradox", and wouldn't tell me. Do you have any idea of what is supposed to happen?'

'Simple enough. Find He and kill him. That should put paid to the entire operation. I've had two tries at him, shooting once and thermite bombs the second, and haven't succeeded. Maybe this will be lucky three.'

'Perhaps you ought to let me take care of him,' Angelina said sweetly.

'A fine idea. We'll blast him together. I have had just about enough of this temporal paper chase.'

'How do we find him?'

'Simplicity itself, if you have a time energy detector with you.' She did, Coypu's foresight, and passed it over. 'A simple flick of this switch and the moving needle points to our man.'

The switch flicked but did nothing more than release a little condensed water that ran out into my palm.

'It doesn't seem to be working,' Angelina said, smiling sweetly.

'Either that or they are not using the time-helix at this particular moment.' I rummaged in my equipment. 'I had to leave my space suit and some other things back in 1807, but Slippery Jim is never without his snooper.'

I was proud of the gadget and had designed it myself, and it was one of the few things He hadn't taken from me. Rugged, it could resist almost anything except being dropped into molten metal. Compact, no bigger than my hand. And it could detect the weakest of flickerings of radiation across a tremendous range of frequencies. I turned it on and ran my finger over the familiar controls.

'Most interesting,' I said, and tried the radio frequencies.

'If you don't enlighten me quick, I'll never save your life again.'

'You have to because you love me with an undying passion. I get two sources, one weak and very distant. The other can't be too far and is putting out on a number of frequencies, including atomic radiation and energy transmission, as well as a lot of radio. And something of more pressing urgency. Get out the sunburn cream – solar ultraviolet radiation is right up at the top of the scale. You can bet I've been well cooked already.'

We creamed and, despite the heat, put on enough clothing to shield us from the invisible radiation that was pouring out of the clouded sky.

'Strange things have happened to the Earth,' I said. 'The radiation, this soggy climate, the wildlife in this river. I wonder—'

'I don't. After completing the mission, you can do your paleogeologic research. Let's kill He first.'

'Spoken like a pro. I hope you don't mind if I rig a harness so we can share the benefit of the grav-chute equally this time?'

'Sounds like fun,' she said, loosening the straps.

The airborne Siamese twin arrangement lifted and took us low over the sea of gunk in the direction of all the activity. Mud and swamp continued for a boringly long time, and I was beginning to chafe in the straps and worry about the power supply when the higher land finally appeared. First some rocks sticking up out of the water, then sheer cliffs. It took more juice to lift us up the side of these, and the indicator on the power pack dropped quickly.

'We are going to have to walk soon,' I said, 'which is at least better than swimming.'

'Not if the land animals match those in the water.'

Ever optimistic my Angelina. As I was phrasing a witty and scathing reply, there was a flash of light from the rampart of rocks ahead, followed instantly by an intense pain in my leg.

'I've been shot!' I shouted, more in surprise than pain, reaching for the grav-chute controls and finding that Angelina had already killed the power.

We dropped toward a wicked jumble of rocks, slowing and stopping only at the last minute. I hopped on one leg to the shelter of an overhanging slab and was thinking of digging out my medikit when Angelina sprayed antiseptic on the wound, tore my pants leg half away, injected instant pain-killer in my thigh, and probed the gory opening. She was ahead of me with everything, and I didn't mind in the slightest.

'A neat penetrating wound,' she announced, spraying on surgifoam. 'Should heal quickly, no problems, keep your weight off it; now I have to kill whoever did it.'

All the drugs had slowed me down, and before I could answer, she had her gun in her hand and had faded silently into the rocky landscape. There is nothing like having a loving and tender wife who is a cool and accomplished killer. Maybe I wore the pants in the family – but we both wore guns.

Not too long after this there was the sound of explosions, a great clattering in the rocks above and, soon after that, some hoarse screams that soon ended in silence. It is a tribute to Angelina's prowess that I never for a second was concerned about her safety. In fact, I dozed off under the assault of the drugs coursing through my bloodstream and woke only when I was aware of tugging on the grav-chute harness. I yawned and blinked at her as she buckled in beside me.

'Am I allowed to ask what happened?' I said. She frowned.

'Just one man up there; I couldn't find any others. There is a farm building of sorts, some machinery, crops growing. I must be slipping. I knocked him out, then could not bring myself to shoot him while he was lying there unconscious.'

I kissed her as we rose.

'A conscience, my sweet. Some of us are born with them; yours was surgically implanted. The results are the same.'

'I'm not really sure I like it. There was a certain freedom in the old days.'

'We all have to be civilized some time.' She sighed and nodded, then gave me a quick peck on the cheek.

'I suppose that you are right. But it would have been so satisfying to blow him into small pieces.'

We were over the last of the tumbled scree now and ascending a small cliff. There was a plateau here on top of which was a low building made of cemented-together stones. The door was open, and I hobbled through it, leaning on Angelina's shoulder. Inside, the dim light through the small windows revealed a large and cluttered room with two bunks against the far wall. On one of them a bound man lay twisting and turning, mumbling and growling into the gag that sealed his mouth.

'You get into the other bed,' Angelina said, 'while I see if I can get any intelligence out of this awful creature.'

I had actually taken the first steps toward the bunk before reason penetrated my soggy thoughts and I stopped dead.

'Beds. Two of them? There must be someone else around the place.'

Whatever answer was on her lips was never spoken because a man appeared in the doorway behind us, shouting noisily and firing an even noisier weapon.

## EIGHTEEN

He was shouting mainly because the weapon was blown from his hands even as he triggered it, and an instant later he was blown back out of the doorway. I saw all this as I dived and rolled and had my gun out just as Angelina was putting hers away.

'Now that is more like it,' she said, apparently addressing the silent pair of boots in the doorway. 'Civilized conscience or no, I find that shooting in self-defense still comes easily. I saw this one out among the rocks, stalking us as we came in, but I never had a clear shot. Everything should be quieter now. I'll make some nice warm soup and you take a nice nap. . . .'

'No.' I doubt if a firmer 'no' had ever been spoken. I popped out a pair of stimtabs and chewed them as I continued my monologue in the same tone of voice. 'There is a certain retrogressive pleasure in being cared for and treated like an idiot child – but I think I have had enough of it. I have tackled He before this and chased him out of two of his lairs and I intend to finish him off now. I know his ways. I'm in charge of this expedition, so you will follow, not lead, and will obey orders.'

'Yes, sir,' she answered with lowered eyelids and bowed head. Did this cover a mocking smile? I did not care. Me boss.

'Me boss.' It sounded even better said aloud in a firm and declaratory tone.

'Yes, boss,' she said and giggled prettily while the man on the bed writhed and chomped and the boots in the doorway were silent.

We went to work. Our prisoner slavered noisily in an unknown tongue when I took out the gag and tried to bite my fingers when I restored it. There was a rough-looking radio on a shelf that produced only grating broadcasts in the same language when I turned it on. Angelina's outdoor investigations were far more productive than mine, and she pulled up by the door in an impossibly ugly conveyance that looked like a scratched, purple, plastic bathtub slung between four sets of wheels. It burbled and hissed at me when I hobbled up to examine it.

'Very simple to operate,' Angelina said, showing off her technical skill. 'There is only one switch and that turns it on. And two handles, one for the bank of wheels on each side. Forward to speed them up, back to brake them . . .'

'And neutral in the middle,' I said to demonstrate *my* technical skill, as well as the fact that I was a male chauvinist pig and this was my show. 'And this lead-covered lump in the rear must be a nuclear generator. Unshield a chunk of radioactive material, heat up the surrounding liquid, a heat exchanger here, secondary liquid to turn this electric generator, motors in each wheel, ugly and crude but practical. Where do we go in it?'

She pointed. 'There seems to be a road or trail of sorts going off through that cultivated field there. And unless memory fails – and I *know* you will be quick to correct me – that seems to be the same direction as the radio signals you detected earlier.'

A mild blow struck for femlib, and I ignored it. Particularly since she was right as the snooper soon confirmed.

'Off we go then,' I said, in command once again.

'Going to kill the prisoner?' she asked hopefully.

'Thank you, no. But I'll take his clothes since mine have reached the old rag stage. If we break up the radio, he'll have a hard job telling anyone we're coming. He'll chew through his gag and ropes in a couple of hours, so we can leave the burial arrangements of his associate to him. We will load our gear and be on our way.'

The firmness of my authority was dimmed slightly by the *krets krets* of my fingernails inside my tattered shirt scratching at the rapid red-blooming growth of my sunburn. While

Angelina stomped the radio, I put on more cream. A few minutes later we were bumping along the well-worn track that twisted across the high plateau.

There was less fog and haze at this altitude, not that there was anything more to see. The rough landscape was quarried with gullies that carried away the water from the frequent rainstorms, also removing what little topsoil still remained. Tough-looking plants clung to the rocks for protection in the sheltered spots. Occasionally we passed a branching off of the wheel marks, but the direction finder on the snooper kept us on the right track. The hard bucket seats were hideously uncomfortable, and I welcomed the gathering darkness of sunset – though of course I didn't say this aloud – and turned off behind a jumbled hill of great rocks for the night.

In the morning I was stiff but feeling more fit. The growth and healing drugs had whipped my cells into a frenzy of growth that had half healed my various wounds and given me a raging appetite. We dined and drank from the meager supplies that Angelina had brought – eked out by some coarse bread and dried meat liberated from the homicidal farmers. Angelina took the wheel and I rode shotgun, not liking the look of the decomposing landscape at all. The track now wandered down from the hills as the highlands turned into a vertical escarpment of rock. Then there were more swamps and some very nasty-looking jungle into which the road dipped. Creepers hung low enough to brush our heads and the soggy trees touched overhead. The air, which did not seem possible, became even more humid and hotter.

'I don't like this place,' Angelina said, steering around a boggy spot that sloped across the track.

'I don't like it even less,' I said, gun in hand and a clip of explosive cartridges in the butt. 'If the wildlife here is anything like that in the river, we could have some fun and games in store.'

Ever alert, I looked ahead, behind, right and left and wished my eyeballs grew on stalks. There were numberless suspicious dark shapes among the trees and occasional heavy crashings could be heard, but nothing appeared to threaten us. That I could see. Of course the one spot I wasn't watching was the surface of the road, and that is where the imminent danger lay.

'That tree has fallen right across the road,' Angelina said. 'Just bump over it—'

'I wouldn't!' I said, just a little bit too late as our wheels trundled over the green trunk that lay across the track and vanished into the jungle on both sides.

Our center wheels were on it when it shuddered and heaved upward in a great loop. The vehicle turned over, and Angelina and I were hurled clear. But not clear enough. I hit the ground and tucked my head in and rolled and came up with the gun ready. A good thing too. The pseudo tree trunk was writhing nicely, while out of the foliage across the track appeared the front end of the thing.

A snake. With a head as big as a barrel, gaping mouth, flicking tongue, beady eyes, hissing like an exploding boiler. While right under those widespread jaws was Angelina, sitting up and shaking her head dizzily and totally unaware of what was happening. There was time for one shot, and I wanted it to be a good one. As that demonic head came down, I held my wrist with my left hand to steady the gun and squeezed off a round right into the thing's mouth. With a muffled thud its head was blown off in a cloud of smoke.

That should have been the end of it – except for a gigantic spasm that went through the entire length of that muscular body. Before I could get out of the way, a shuddering thrashing loop struck me, bowled me over, and hurled me into the trees. This time there was no fancy roll and dive but a simple crunch splintery bang as I crashed through the branches, and one got me on the side of the head, and with a nice white explosion of pain that was that.

A period of time passed that I was not aware of. It was the ache in my head that drew me reluctantly back to consciousness, plus a new and sharper pain in my leg. I opened one bleary eye and saw something small and brown with a lot of claws and teeth that was tearing an opening in my pants leg in order to make lunch out of my thigh. The first hungry bite was what had woken me, and before it could go on to a second course, I kicked it with my boot. It growled and screeched at this and showed me all its teeth but reluctantly slipped away into the foliage when I attempted another weak kick in its direction.

Weak was the word for everything I felt. It took me some time to do more than lie there and gasp and try to remember what had happened. The road, the snake, the wreck. . . .

'Angelina!' I shouted hoarsely and struggled to my feet, ignoring the waves of pain that washed through me. 'Angelina!'

There was no answer. I pushed through the shrubbery to witness a singularly nasty sight. A churning row of brown animals, relatives of the one who had nibbled me, were working on the carcass of the snake and had already reduced great sections of it to neatly polished rib cage. And my gun was gone. I turned back and searched where I had fallen, but it was not there. Something was wrong, very wrong, and the shrill voice of panic was beginning to keen in the back of my head.

As long as I stayed clear of them, the carrion eaters ignored me, so I made a wide circle across the road. The car was gone as well. And so was Angelina.

This required cogent thought which was impossible with the aches and pains that were crippling me. And I had to do something about the insects that were buzzing about the wound in my head. My medikit was still in its pocket and that was next in the order of business. In a few minutes I was soothed, depained, stimulated, and ready for action. But where was the action? Wherever the car was, my clicking thoughts responded. Its tracks were clear enough in the muddy ground – which also revealed the mystery of Angelina's disappearance. There were at least two sets of large, ugly masculine footprints around the churned area where the vehicle had been righted. As well as another set of car tracks. Either we had been followed or a chance bunch of tourists had arrived on the scene after the snake incident. Spatters of mud and bent grass showed that both cars had carried on in the original direction we had been going. I went that way myself, in a ground-eating trot, trying not to think about what might have happened to Angelina.

This trotting didn't last long. The heat and fatigue slowed me to a shambling walk. A stimtab took care of one, and I just sweated out the other. The tracks were clear, and I followed. In less than an hour the road had wound its way up out of the jungle and into the dry hills. Coming around a turn, I had a quick glimpse of one of the cars pulled up ahead and I drew quickly back.

A plan was needed. My gun had vanished, so shooting down the kidnappers was slightly out of the question. The few remaining devices in my clothing were nonlethal, though I did have a wrist holder full of grenades that Angelina had given me. This was the answer. A handful of sleepgas bombs to drop the kidnappers before they could shoot me. And maybe a couple of explosive grenades in the other hand just in case any of the enemy were not near Angelina and needed more dramatic means of disposal.

Thus armed and ready, I crept forward from rock to rock, took a deep breath, and jumped into the clearing where both vehicles waited.

And caught the wooden club in the side of my head, wielded by the guard who had been waiting quietly for someone to pull this kind of stunt.

# NINETEEN

I was only out a fraction of a second, long enough for my wrists and ankles to be tied and all my weapons that they could find to be stripped from me. For this disaster I can blame only myself and my inattention. Fatigue and stimulants may have contributed, but my own stupidity had been the cause. I cursed myself under my breath, which did no good at all, as I was dragged across the ground and dumped down by Angelina.

'Are you all right?' I croaked.

'Of course. And in far better shape than you are.'

Which was true. Her clothing was torn and there were some bruises where she had been knocked around. Someone was going to pay and pay well for that. I could hear my teeth grating together. And she was tied just as I was.

'They thought you were dead,' she said. 'And so did I.' There was a wealth of unsaid feeling in her words, and I tried a smile which was a little more twisted than I like. 'I don't know how long we lay there; I was unconscious, too. When I came to, I was like this, and they had taken the guns and everything and were loading it all into the cars. Then we left. There was nothing I could do to stop them. All they speak is that same horrible language.'

They looked as horrible as their language sounded, all scruffy clothing and greasy leather straps, bushels of matted dirty hair and beard. I had an entirely unnecessary closer look at one of them when he came over and twisted my head to one side and the other while he compared my crunched features with a good photograph of myself that he had. I snapped my teeth at the filthy fingers, but he pulled them away in time. These must be He's men; the photo proved that, though I had no idea where He got it from. Taken during one of our tangles in time, no doubt, and treasured in his pocket ever since. At this point I noticed the ugliest and smelliest of the lot ogling Angelina, and I snapped at his ankle and was kicked aside for my pains.

Give Angelina that, she is a very direct-minded girl. When she knows what she wants, she gets it, no matter what. Now she saw the only way we could get out of this mess and she used it. Woman's wiles. With no hint of disgust at the ugly brute she lavished her attentions upon. She could not speak their language, but the language she did speak was as old as mankind. Turning away from me, she smiled at the hairy beast and gave a twist of her head to call him over. Her shoulders were back, her charming figure prominent, her hips tilted coyly.

Of course it worked. There was a bit of lively discussion with the other two, but Hairiest knocked one of them down, and that was that. They looked on with burning jealousy as he stalked over to her. She smiled her warmest and held out her slim, bound wrists.

What man could resist that unspoken appeal? Certainly not this shambling hulk. He cut the thongs on her wrists and put his knife away as she bent to free her ankles. When he hauled her to her feet, she arose eagerly. He locked her in a bearlike embrace, bending his face to hers.

I could have told him that he would be safer off trying to kiss a saber-tooth tiger, but I did not. What happened next only I could see because the jealous watchers were blocked from sight by the bulk of his body. Who would imagine that those delicate fingers could shape themselves into that hard a point, that the thin wrist could propel the hand so deep into bushy's gut? Lovely. He bent to her and, with only a gentle sigh, kept bending. For a moment she supported his weight – then stepped back and screamed as he folded to the ground.

A picture of feminine innocence, hands to cheeks, eyes staring, shrieking at the strange occurrence of a strong man collapsing at her feet. Of course the other two ran over, but there were the beginnings of expressions of cold suspicion on their faces. The first one carried my gun.

Angelina took care of him. As soon as he was close enough and bringing up the gun, she let fly with bushy's knife that she had removed before she dropped him. I did not see where it hit because the third man was passing me and I had drawn my legs back in hopes that he would. He did. I kicked out and got him below the knees, and he went down. Even as he fell I was jackknifing forward, and before he could get up again, I let him have it with both boots in the side of the head. And a second time just because I was feeling nasty.

That was that. Angelina removed the knife from her un-moving target, wiped it on his clothing, then came to free me.

'Will you kill the ones who are still twitching?' she asked demurely.

'I should, but cold-blooded revenge is not for me either. They are what they are, and I suppose that is penalty enough. I think if we took all their supplies and wrecked their wagon, it would be revenge enough. You were wonderful.'

'Of course. That's why you married me.' She kissed me quickly because she had to turn an instant later to land her heel on the forehead of bushy, who was beginning to twitch. He slept on. We packed and left.

Our goal was not too far away. A few hours later we felt a stirring of the air that grew stronger as we continued down the track through the hills. A sudden turn brought us to the brink of a valley with a sharp drop, and I kicked the vehicle into a swirling spin and darted it back out of sight again.

'Did you see that?' I asked.

'I certainly did,' Angelina replied as we slipped forward on our bellies, more cautiously this time and looked around the turn.

The wind was stronger here, pouring up the wide valley from some invisible source below. The air was cooler, too, and though there were the ever-present clouds above, there was no fog in the valley to obscure the view. Across from us the hill rose, turning to a solid cliff that reared up vertically, glossy black stone. Erosion had carved it into a fantasy of towers and turrets; men had carved these further into a castle city that covered the mountaintop.

There were windows and doorways, flags and pennants, stairs and buttresses. The flags were bright red inscribed with half-seen black characters. Some of the towers had been painted crimson as well, and this, with the mad frenzy of the construction, meant only one thing.

'It's not logical, I know,' Angelina said. 'But that place sends a definite shiver down my spine. It seems, hard to describe, perhaps insane is the best word.'

'The absolute best. Which means that since this is the right world and time, a place that looks like that must be where He is.'

'How do we get to him?'

'A very good question,' I said in lieu of an intelligent answer. How *did* we get into this kooky castle? I scratched my head and rubbed my jaw, but these infallible aids to thought did not work this time. There was a slight movement at the edge of my vision, and I looked and grabbed for my gun – and froze the motion halfway.

'Don't make any sudden motions, particularly in the direction of your weapon,' I told Angelina in a quiet voice. 'Turn around slowly.'

We both did. Doing nothing that might produce anxiety in the trigger fingers of the dozen or so men who had appeared silently behind us and stood with leveled and firmly aimed weapons.

'Get ready to dive forward when I do,' I said and turned back to see another four men who had appeared just as silently in the valley just in front of us. 'Belay that last command, and smile sweetly and surrender. We'll chop them up after we get in among them.'

This last was meant more as a morale booster than an assurance of action. Unlike the wild-eyed men from whom we had taken our multiwheeled transportation, this lot was much cooler and firmer. They were dressed alike in gray one-piece plastic outfits that turned into hoods to cover their heads. Their weapons were as long as rifles, gape-orificed and lethal-looking. We trotted forward obediently when one of them waved that instruction in our direction. Another member of the closing circle stepped closer and looked us over, but not close enough for anyone who wasn't suicide-prone to attempt to seize his weapon.

'*Stragitzkruml?*' he said, then continued when we remained silent.

'*Fidlykreepi?*'

'*Attentottenpotentaten?*'

When there was no response to these incomprehensible requests, he turned to a bulky man with a red beard who seemed to be in charge.

'*Ili ne parolas konantajn lingvojn,*' he said in clearly accented Esperanto.

'Well, that's more like it,' I answered in the same tongue. 'Might I ask why you gentlemen find it necessary to pull guns on simple travelers like ourselves?'

'Who are you?' Red-beard said, coming forward.

'I might ask the same of you?'

'*I* am pointing the guns,' he answered coldly.

'A well-made point and I bow to your logic. We are tourists from the land across the sea. . . .' He interrupted with a short and nasty word.

'That is impossible as we both know since this is the only landmass on this planet. The truth now.'

We both hadn't known, though we did now. A single continent? What had happened to Mother Earth during those twenty millennia? Lying had been no good, so perhaps the truth might work. It did upon occasion.

'Would you believe me if I told you we were time travelers?'

This hit the target all right, and he looked startled, while there was a stir of movement among the men close enough to hear what I had said. Red-beard glared them into silence before he spoke again.

'What is your connection with He and those creatures in his city up there?'

A lot depended upon my answer. Truth had worked once,

and it might turn the trick again. And he had said 'creatures', which was a give-away. I couldn't believe this calm and disciplined force could be associated with the enemy.

'I have come to kill He and wipe out his operation.'

This really did produce the right effect, and some of the men even lowered their guns before being growled back into line. Red-beard muttered a command, and one of the men hurried off. We remained in silence until he returned with a green metal cube about the size of his head that he handed over to the commander. It must have been hollow because he carried it easily. Red-beard held it up.

'We have over a hundred of these. They have been floating down out of the sky for the past month, and all of them are identical. A powerful radio source inside leads us to them – but we cannot cut or dissolve the metal. On the outside, on five faces of the cube, they are covered with lines of writing in what appear to be different languages and scripts. The ones we can translate all read the same way. Bring this to the time travelers. On the bottom of the cube are two lines of writing that we cannot read. Can you?'

He slowly held out the cube toward me, and I took it just as gingerly as every gun was trained on my body with careful precision. The metal looked like collapsium, the incredibly tough stuff used for atomic rocket tube liners. I carefully turned it bottom up and read the lines in a single glance before handing it back.

'I can read them,' I said, and they were aware of the new tone in my voice. 'The first line says that He and his people will all leave this period exactly 2.37 days after my arrival here.'

There was a murmur over that, and Angelina beat Red-beard to the punch with the important question.

'What was in the second line?'

I tried a smile, but it didn't seem much good.

'Oh, that. It says that the planet will be destroyed by atomic explosions as soon as they go.'

## TWENTY

The tent was made of the same gray fabric as the clothes our captors wore and was a chilled refuge from the steambath atmosphere outside. A squat machine whirred in one corner, dehumidifying and cooling the air. Even cooler drinks had been produced, and I drained and brooded over mine, trying to see a way out of this dilemma before the deadly deadline was reached. Though guns were still in evidence, an unspoken truce was in effect; Red-beard decided to formalize it.

'I drink with you,' he said. 'I am Diyan.'

It seemed very much like a ritual, so I repeated the formula and introduced myself, as did Angelina. After this the weapons vanished, and we were all much more chummy. I sat down where I could benefit from the full breeze of the cooler and decided to ask some questions myself.

'Do you people have any weapons heavier than these handguns?'

'None that are available. The few we brought have been destroyed in battle with He's forces.'

'Is this continent so big you can't get more of them here quickly from your country?'

'The size of the continent is of no importance. Our space vessels are very small, and everything must be brought from our home planet.'

I blinked rapidly, feeling I was getting out of my depth.

'You are not from Earth?' I asked.

'Our ancestors were, but we are all native-born Martians.'

'You wouldn't care to give me a *few* more facts, would you? The sound of confusion I keep hearing appears to be inside my own head.'

'I am sorry, I thought you knew. Here, let me fill up your glass. The story really begins many thousands of years ago when a sudden change in solar radiation raised the temperature here on Earth. By sudden I of course mean a matter of years, really centuries. As the climate changed and the ice caps melted, the continued existence of life on the surface of the planet was threatened. Coastlines were altered and immense areas of low-lying land inundated; great cities were drowned. This in itself might have been dealt with had it not been for the seismic disturbances brought about by the shifting weight on the Earth's surface as the poles were freed of their ice burden and the released water covered other areas. Earthquakes and lava flows, sinking lands and the rising of new mountains. All quite terrible, we have seen the recordings many times in our schools. An incredible international effort was launched to terrafy the planet Mars – that is, make it suitable for human habitation. This involved the creation of an atmosphere there with a high carbon dioxide layer to trap the increased radiation of the sun, the transportation of ice mountains from the rings of Saturn, things like this. It was a noble ambition that in the end did succeed, but it bankrupted the nations of Earth who gave their all in this unbelievable effort. Eventually there was dissent and even warfare as weakened governments fell and greedy men fought for more than an equal share of space on the new-made world. Through all this the waters continued to rise on Earth and the first Martian settlers struggled against the harsh rigors of a barely livable world to establish the settlements. In history these are known as the Deadly Years because so many people died; the figures are unbelievable. But in the end we survived, and Mars is a green and comfortable world.

'Earth did not fare as well. Contact was lost between the planets, and the survivors of the once-teeming billions here fought a dreadful battle for survival. There are no written records of that period, thousands of years long, but the results are clear enough. This single large continent remained above the sea, as well as some island chains to mark earlier mountain ranges. And madness rules mankind. When we were able, we rebuilt the ancient spaceships and brought what help we could. Our help was not appreciated. The survivors kill strangers on sight and take great pleasure in it. And all men are strangers. The almost-unshielded solar radiation here produced mutants of all kinds among man, plants and animals. Most mutations died off quickly, but the survivors are deadly to a universal degree. So we helped where we could but really did very little. The earthmen were a continuing danger to each other but not to Mars. That is not until He united them some hundreds of years ago.'

'Has he really lived all that time?'

'It appears that he has. His mind is as bent as theirs, but he can communicate with them. They follow him. They actually work together, building that city you have seen, building a society of sorts. He is certainly a genius, albeit a warped one, and they have factories going and a rudimentary technology. The first thing they did was ask for more aid from Mars and would not believe us when we said that they were getting the maximum already. Their mad demands would not have bothered us had they not unearthed rockets armed with atomic bombs that could be directed at our planet. It was after the first of these arrived that this expedition was organized. On Mars we survived by cooperating, there was no other way, so we are not a warlike people. But we have made weapons and will reluctantly use them to ensure our own survival. He is the key to all the troubles, and we must capture or kill him. If we must kill others to accomplish this, we will do that as well. Thousands are dead at home and radioactivity is increasing in the Martian atmosphere.'

'Then our aims are identical.' I told him. 'He has launched a time attack against our people with equally disastrous results. You have summed up our retaliatory plans quite neatly.'

'How do we go about it?' Diyan asked eagerly.

'I'm not sure,' I answered gloomily.

'We have a little over ten standard hours left to operate in,' Angelina said, precisely. Like all women, she was a true pragmatist. While we wasted time nattering about the past, she faced the fact that the decision would have to be made in the future and tackled that, the real problem. I yearned to demonstrate my affection for her but decided that would have to wait for a more appropriate time, if more time did exist at all.

'An all-out attack,' I said. 'We have weapons we can add to yours. Attack on all fronts, find a weak spot, concentrate our forces, blast through to victory. Do you have any large weapons left?'

'No.'

'Well . . . we can get around that. How about crash-landing one of your spacers inside the castle up there, get a fighting force behind their backs that way?'

'All of them were destroyed by saboteurs, suicidal ones. Others are coming from Mars but will arrive too late. We are not really very good at war and killing while they have always lived with it.'

'Not to give up hope yet, ha-ha.' I laughed, but it had a very hollow ring to it. The dark gloom was so thick in the air you could have cut chunks of it out.

'The grav-chute,' Angelina said quietly so only I heard her.

'We will use the grav-chute,' I said loudly so all could hear. A good general depends on able staffwork. The complete plan was now clear, written in letters of fire before my eyes.

'This is a go-for-broke operation. Angelina and I are going to drain the charges from all our unessential equipment to put a full charge into the grav-chute. Then we will rig a multiple harness for this. I'll do the exact computations later, but I would guess that it will lift five or six people up over those walls and inside before it burns out. Angelina and I are two, the rest will be your best people. . . .'

'A woman, no, this is not work for a woman,' Diyan protested. I patted his arm understandingly.

'Have no fear. Sweet and demure as she is, she can outfight any ten men in this tent. And everyone is needed. Because the troops outside will be launching a *very* realistic attack that might break through. General at first, then concentrating on one flank. When the noise is at its highest, the commando squad will lift over the opposite wall and bore in. Now let's get things organized.'

We got things organized. Or rather Angelina and I did because these peaceful Martian plowboys knew but nothing about scientific slaughter and were only too happy to turn the responsibilities of leadership over to us. Once things were under way I lay down for a quick sleep – I had been awake or clubbed unconscious something like two full days and 20,000 years, so was understandably tired. The three hours I grabbed were certainly not enough, and I awoke chomping and blinking and chewed a stimtab to make up the difference. It was dark outside the tent and still just as hot.

'Are we ready to roll?' I asked.

'Any minute now,' Angelina said, cool and relaxed and showing no signs of her labors; she must have been at the stimtabs, too. 'We have about four hours to dawn, and we will need most of that to get into position. The attack begins at first light.'

'Do the guides know the way?'

'They have been fighting in and around this position for almost a year now, so they should.'

This was the showdown. The men were all aware of it. It was there in the set of their faces and the brace of their shoulders. There could be only one winner this day. Perhaps they weren't born fighters, but they were learning fast. If you are going to fight, you fight to win. Diyan came up leading three more of his men who carried the jury-rigged metal harness with the grav-chute built into the center of it.

'We are ready,' he said.

'Everyone knows what he is to do?'

'Perfectly. We have already said our good-byes and the first attack units have moved out.'

'Then we'll get going, too.'

Diyan led the way, though how he found it in that steam-heated darkness I have no idea. We stumbled along behind him, sweating and cursing under the burden of the clumsy harness, and the less said about the following hours, the better. Dawn found us collapsed under the far wall, the highest and apparently the strongest, that was our target. As it appeared out of the haze above us, black and grim, it did not look at all attractive. I squeezed Angelina's hand to show her I was fearless and to cheer her up. She squeezed mine back to show that she knew I was just as frightened as the rest of them.

'We'll do it, Jim,' she said. 'You know that.'

'Oh, we'll do it all right; the continuing existence of our particular hunk of the future proves that. But it doesn't indicate how many are going to die today – or which of us will live on into the foreseeable future.'

'We're immortal,' she said with such surety that I had to laugh and my morale soared up to its usual egotistical heights, and I kissed her soundly and well for the aid.

Explosions sounded suddenly in the distance, rumbling and rolling like thunder from the rock walls. The attack had begun. The clock was running and everything was timed from here on in. I helped everyone strap in and kept an eye on my watch at the same time. As our scheduled hop-off drew close, I buckled in as well and touched the grav-chute controls.

'Brace yourselves,' I said, watching the numbers flutter by. 'And be ready to cut free when we hit at the other end.'

I hit the button, and with a metallic groan from the harness my little force of six rose into the air to the attack.

# TWENTY-ONE

We drifted up the black face of the rock like a slow elevator, sitting ducks for anyone with a good gun and a keen eye. It was uncomfortable to say the least. I had to lift off gradually so our harness wouldn't buckle, but I speeded up as fast as I could until we were on maximum lift. A visible aura of heat began to radiate from the grav-chute as it struggled against all our dead weight. It would be highly uncomfortable if it failed now.

Then deep-cut windows flashed by, happily unoccupied, and the black stone changed to dark wall and the crenellated top of the parapet was ahead. I angled toward it and cut the power completely just before we reached the edge. Our acceleration carried us up and over in a high arc, and after that, things happened at an incredibly rapid pace.

There were two guards on the wall, both surprised, angry, armed, about to fire. But Angelina and I fired first. We were using the needle guns now in order to remain undetected as long as possible. The guards crumpled in silence, their faces and necks suddenly bristly as pincushions, and I hit the power on for the landing.

Landing! There was no courtyard or solid roof below! We were coming down on a domed and transparent cover over a large workshop, a canopy made of what appeared to be glass panels held in a tangled web of rusty metal braces. We looked at it, horrified, as we rushed toward it, and I had the power on to the last stop. We groaned at the sudden acceleration, and the harness groaned as well and creaked and bent. The dome was too close, and we were just not going to stop in time.

It was lovely. A silent, secret attack, flitting gray ghosts in the dawn. Six pairs of boots hit at the same instant, and about five thousand square meters of glass were kicked out. The supporting framework twanged and bent, and some of the rusty supports snapped free. For one shuddering instant I thought we were going to follow all the glass that was now crashing and clashing into the chamber below with a hideously loud cacophony. Then the grav-chute gave its all with one shuddering last blaze of energy, halting our forward motion, then burst into flame as well.

'Grab the supports!' I shouted, tearing at the buckles that held the grav-chute to our harness. It resisted, searing my hand, then finally dropped free. Straight down into the hall with its screaming occupants below, where it promptly exploded. I sighed and dropped some smoke and fire bombs as well to add to the confusion.

'Our presence is now known,' I said, inching back toward safety. 'I suggest we get off this precarious jungle gym and back on the job.'

Moving carefully, sending more glass crashing down as our weight bent the frame out of place and the panes slipped free, we crept back to the safety of the parapet.

'Get on the radio,' I told Diyan as he climbed up next to me. 'Tell your troops to pull back their attack if they haven't broken in but to keep up the firing.'

'They have been repulsed on all sides.'

'Then tell them to cut their losses, We'll do the blitz from the inside.'

We moved out. Angelina and I on the point where we could blast any resistance that appeared, while the others protected our flanks and rear. Forward at a sweaty trot. We had to move fast, sow discord as we went – and find He. The first door opened onto a great circular staircase that seemed to spiral down to infinity. I didn't like the looks of it, so I rolled some concussion grenades down it, and we pressed on across the roof.

'Where to?' Angelina asked.

'That tangle of turrets and buildings up ahead seems to be

larger and more functional than most of this place. As good a guess as any.' Something exploded on the tiles nearby, and Angelina picked the sniper out of a window above with a single snap shot from the waist. We ran a bit faster, then pressed against the wall above a straight drop to the valley below while I blew out a locked door. Then we were in.

The place had been designed by a madman. I know that is literally true, but you didn't have to know He to get the message. Corridors and stairs, twisted chambers, angled walls, even one spot where we had to crawl on our hands and knees under the low ceiling. This was where we had our first casualty. Five of us were clear of this room before the ceiling silently and swiftly descended and crushed the rear guard before he could even make a sound. We all were sweating harder. The enemy we met were not armed for the most part and either fled or were dropped by our needle guns. It was speed and silence now, and we moved as fast as we could between the bizarrely decorated walls, finding it easy to avoid looking at the incredible paintings that seemed to cover every square meter of available space.

'Just one moment,' Angelina panted, pulling me to a stop as we came through a high archway to a staircase that spiraled out of sight below, each stone step being a different height from the others. 'Do you know where we are going?'

'Not exactly,' I panted in return. 'Just penetrating the establishment to get ahead of the fighting, while spreading a bit of confusion.'

'I thought we had bigger ambitions. Like finding He.'

'Any suggestions how we might go about that?' I am forced to admit that I snapped a bit as I said that. Angelina responded with saccharine sweetness.

'Why, yes. You might try turning on the time energy detector you have slung around your neck. I believe that is the reason we brought it.'

'Just what I was going to do anyway,' I said, lying to conceal the fact that I had forgotten completely about it in the white heat of the rampaging attack.

The needle swung about and pointed with exact precision to the floor beneath our feet.

'Down and down we go,' I ordered. 'Where the time-helix coils there will be found the He whom I am about to make into mincemeat.' I meant it too since this was the third and last try. I had constructed a special bomb on which I had painted his name. It was a hellish mixture of a curdler – guaranteed to coagulate all protein within five meters – an explosive charge, a load of poisoned shrapnel, and a thermite bomb theoretically to cook the curdled, coagulated, poisoned body of He.

After this the fighting picked up. Some sort of flame-thrower below sent a wave of roiling smoke and fire up the stairs toward us that we could not pass. Singed and smoking, we went out through a hole I blasted in the wall and dropped into a laboratory of sorts. Row after row of bubbling retorts stretched away in all directions, hooked to a maze of crystal plumbing. Dark liquids dripped, and valves hissed foul-smelling steam. The workers here weren't armed, and they dropped before us. We were trotting slower now and gasping for breath.

'Uggh!' Angelina said, making a twisted face. 'Have you seen just what is in those jars?'

'No, and I don't want to. Press on.' Anything that could bother the ice-cool Angelina was something I had no desire to see at all. I was glad when we left this area behind and found another stairwell.

We were getting close. Resistance kept firming up, and we had to battle most of the way now. Only the fact that the defenders were haphazardly armed allowed us to get through at all. Apparently most of the weapons were at use on the walls because these people came at us with knives, axes, lengths of metal, anything and everything. Including their bare hands if that was all they had. Screaming and frothing, they rushed to the attack and slowed us just by the weight of their numbers. We had our next casualty when a man with a metal spike dropped from some cranny above and stabbed one of the Martians before I could shoot him. They died together, and all we could do was leave them and push on. I took a quick look at my watch and broke into a tired trot again. We were running out of time.

'Wait!' Diyan called out hoarsely. 'The needle, it no longer points.'

I waved everyone to a stop in a wide passage we were traversing, and they dropped, covering the flanks. I looked at the time energy detector that Diyan had been carrying.

'Which way was it pointing when you looked at it last?'

'Straight ahead, down the corridor. And there was no angle to the needle at all, as though this machine it points to were on this level.'

'It only works when the time-helix is operating. It must be off now.'

'Could He have gone?' Angelina asked, speaking aloud the words I was trying to keep out of my thoughts.

'Probably not,' I said with mock sincerity. 'In any case we have to push on as long as we can. One last effort now, dead ahead.'

We pushed. And had another casualty when we attempted to cross a layer of writhing branches that were covered with thorns. Tipped with poison. I finally had to burn the stuff with our last thermite grenade. Ammunition and grenades were running very short. There was a brisk fire fight at the next corridor junction that emptied my needle gun. I tossed it aside and kicked the heavy door that barred any more progress in this direction. It would have to be blown open, and my grenades were exhausted. I turned to Angelina just as a communication plate next to the door lit up.

'You have lost, the final time,' He said, grinning wickedly at me from the screen.

'I'm always willing to talk,' I said, then spoke to Angelina in a language I was sure He did not speak. 'Any concussion grenades left?'

'I am talking, you will listen,' He said.

'One,' Angelina told me.

'I'm all ears,' I said to him. 'Take that door out,' I said to her.

'I have dispatched all the people I need to a safe place in the past where we will never be found. I have sent the machines we will need, I have sent everything that will be needed to build a time-helix as well. I am the last to go, and when I leave, the time machinery will be destroyed behind me.'

The grenade exploded, but the door was thick and remained stuck in the frame. Angelina sprayed it with explosive bullets. He talked on as though this weren't happening.

'I know who you are, little man from the future, and I know where you come from. Therefore I shall destroy you before you have a chance to be born. I will destroy you, my only enemy; then the past and the future and all eternity will be mine, mine, *mine!*'

He was screaming and slavering before he finished, and the door went down, and I was the first one through.

My bullets were exploding in the delicate machinery of the time-helix as my He-bomb arced through the air.

But he had already actuated the time-helix. Its green glow was gone; He was gone, the machinery left behind no longer needed. My hell-bomb exploded in empty air and was more of a danger to us than to the vanished one it had been intended for. We dropped to the floor as death whizzed overhead, and when we looked next, the machinery was dissolving and smoking.

He spoke again, and the muzzle of my gun looked for him.

'I made this recording in case I had to leave abruptly, so sorry.' He chuckled insanely at his own bad humor. 'I have gone now; you cannot follow me, but I can follow you through time. And destroy you. But you have other enemies with you, and I wish them to feel my vengeance, too. They will die, you will all die, everything will die; I control worlds, eternity, destroy worlds. I will destroy this Earth. I leave you only enough time to consider and suffer. You cannot escape.

'In one hour every nuclear weapon on this planet will be triggered.'

'Earth will be destroyed.'

# TWENTY-TWO

There was very little satisfaction to be gained from blowing up the recording machine that had He's hateful voice coiled in its guts, but I did it anyway, one shot. The thing exploded in a cloud of plastic bits and electronic components, and the insane laughter was cut off in mid-cackle. Angelina patted my hand.

'You did your best,' she said.

'But just not good enough. I'm sorry I got you involved in this.'

'I wouldn't want it any other way. What happens to us happens together.'

'This sounds like something very terrible will be done to your people,' Diyan said. 'I am very sorry.'

'Nothing to feel sorry about. We're all in the same boat.'

'In one sense, yes. One hour from now. But Mars is saved, and we who die here know that we accomplished at least that much. Our families and our people will live on.'

'I wish I could say the same,' I said with utmost gloom, borrowing his gun and picking off two of the enemy who tried to rush in through the broken door. 'When we lost here, we lost for all time. I'm surprised we are still around at all, should have snuffed out like candles.'

'Isn't there anything we can do?' Angelina asked. I shrugged.

'Nothing I can think of. You can't outrun H-bombs. The time-helix equipment is kind of melted, so that is out. What we need is a new time-helix, which we are not going to get unless one appears out of thin air.'

In echo to my words there was the sudden crack of displaced air above, and I rolled and ducked, thinking it was a new attack. It wasn't. It was a large green metal case that hung, unsupported in midair. Angelina looked at me in the strangest manner possible.

'If that is a time-helix, you must tell me how you did it.'

For once in my outspoken life I was silent, even more so when the box began to drift down before us, and just before it grounded, I read the lettering on the side.

'Time-helix – open with care.'

I didn't move. It all seemed too unbelievable. The two grav-chutes strapped to the top of the case, the timing device that had caused them to lower the whole thing to the floor, the small recording apparatus also fixed to the case with the boldly lettered words 'Play me' lettered across it. I boggled and gaped and it was ever-practical Angelina who stepped forward and pressed the starting button. Professor Coypu's rotund voice rolled out to us.

'I suggest you get moving rather quickly. The bombs, you know, go off quite soon. I have been asked to tell you, Jim, that the bomb control apparatus is concealed in a cabinet on the far wall behind the dehydrated rations. It has been disguised to look like a portable radio because it really is a portable radio. With additions. If mishandled, it will set all the bombs off now. Which would be uncomfortable. You are to set the three dials to the numbers six six six, which I believe, is the number of the beast. Set them in sequence from right to left. When they have been set, press the *off* button. Now turn me off until you have done that. Be quick about it.'

'All right, all right,' I said, irritated and switched him off. He had quite a commanding tone for an individual who wouldn't be born for another 10,000 years or so. And how come he knew so much? I complained, but I went and did the job, hurling the dehydrated rations to the floor, where they obviously belonged. They looked like lengths of yellowish-green desiccated octopus tentacles. Suckers and all. The radio was there. I did not attempt to move it but set the dials as instructed and pressed the button. Nothing happened.

'Nothing happened,' I said.

'Which is just the way we want it,' Angelina said, standing

on tiptoe to give an appreciative kiss on the cheek. 'You have saved the world.'

Feeling very proud of myself, I swaggered back to the recorder before the admiring gazes of the Martians and switched it on again.

'Don't think you have saved the world,' Coypu said. Party pooper. 'You have just averted its destruction for approximately twenty-eight days. Once activated, the bombs wait that period, then self-destruct. But your Martian associates can profit from this delay. I believe they have supply ships on the way?'

'Due in fifteen days,' Diyan said, hushed awe in his voice at the disembodied oracular powers before him.

'Fifteen days, more than enough time. The Earth will be destroyed, but when its present condition is considered, this is more of a blessing than a tragedy. It is time to open this case now. On top of the controls is a molecular disrupter. If this is pointed at the outside wall, where the small windows are high up, and angled downward at fifteen degrees, it will cut a tunnel that will exit outside the walls. I suggest this be done as soon as possible. The Martians can get out that way. Now press button A, and the time-helix will form. James, Angelina, strap on the grav-chutes and leave as soon as the ready light comes on.'

Still partially unbelieving I did as instructed. The time-helix crackled into existence and groaned and sparked as it wound itself up. Diyan stepped forward, his hand out to take mine.

'We will never forget you or what you have done for our world. Generations yet unborn will read your name and about your exploits in their schoolbooks.'

'Are you sure you have the spelling right?' I asked.

'You make light of this because you are a great and humble man.' First time I have ever been accused of *that*. 'A statue will be erected with "James di Griz, World Saver" inscribed upon it.'

Each Martian shook my hand in turn; it was very embarrassing. There was an admiring gleam in Angelina's eye as well, but women are simple creatures and enjoy basking even in reflected attention. Then the ready light came on, and after a few more good-byes, we put on the grav-chutes as directed and – for the last time I sincerely hoped – were bathed in the cool fire of the time force. Our contact must have triggered the apparatus because before I could make the very apropos remark that was on my lips everything went *zoinng*.

No worse than any other time trip, certainly no better. This was one kind of transportation I would never get adjusted to. Stars like speeding bullets, spiral galaxies whirling around like fireworks, movement that was no movement, time that was no time, all the usual things. The only thing that was good about the trip was its ending, which was in the gymnasium of the Special Corps base, the largest open chamber there. We floated in midair, my Angelina and I, smiling madly at each other and oblivious to the cries of amazement from the sweating athletes below. We held hands in the simple happiness of knowledge that the future still lay ahead of us.

'Welcome home,' she said, and that was really all there was to say.

We floated down, waving to our friends and ignoring their questions for the moment. Coypu and the time lab first, to report. There was a quick feeling of unhappiness that He had escaped me and the hope that this time, when he was tracked through time, a few very large bombs could be sent in the place of me or any other volunteer.

Coypu looked up and gaped. 'What are you doing here?' he said. 'You are supposed to be eliminating this He person. Didn't you get my message?'

'Message?' I asked, blinking rapidly.

'Yes. We made ten thousand metal cubes and sent them back to Earth. Sure you would get one of them. Radio direction and such.'

'Oh, *that* old message. Received and acted upon, but you

are a little out of date. What is that doing here?' I'm afraid my voice rose a bit on this last as I pointed with vibrating finger at the compact machine across the room.

'That? Our Mark One compact folding time-helix? What else should it be doing? We have just finished it.'

'You've never used it?'

'Never.'

'Well, you are now. You have to strap a couple of grav-chutes to it – here, use these – and a recorder and molecular disrupter and shoot it right back to save Angelina and me.'

'I have a pocket recorder, but why . . .' He took a familiar-looking machine from his lab coat.

'Do it first, explanations later. Angelina and I are about to be blown up if you don't do this right.'

I grabbed some paint and wrote 'Play me' on the recorder, then 'Time-helix – open with care' on the machine. The exact moment when He had left Earth was determined by the time tracer and the arrival for this cargo set for a few minutes later on the big helix. Coypu dictated the tape under my instruction, and it wasn't until the whole bundle was whisked back into the past that I heaved a grateful sigh of relief.

'We are saved,' I said. 'Now for that drink you promised me.'

'I didn't promise . . .'

'I'll have it anyway.'

Coypu was muttering to himself and scratching on a pad while I prepared some hefty drinks for Angelina and myself. We clunked glasses and were baptizing our throats when he came over, smiling genially.

'I needed that,' I said. 'It must be *ages* since I last had a drink.'

'It is all coming clear at last,' Coypu said, tapping his protruding teeth with contained excitement.

'Is it all right if we sit while we listen? It's been a busy couple of thousand years.'

'Yes, by all means. Let me retrace the course of events. A time attack was launched upon the Corps by He, a most successful one. Our numbers were quite reduced. . . .'

'Yes, like down to two. You and me.'

'Quite right. Though as soon as I had dispatched you to the year 1975, I found that all things were as they had been. Most sudden. All alone one instant, the next the laboratory full of people who never knew they had been gone. We put a lot of work in on improving the time-tracking techniques, took almost four years to get it the way we wanted.'

'Did you say *four* years?'

'Nearer five before we got it operational. The trails were distant and hard to follow, most tangled as well.'

'Angelina!' I cried with sudden realization. 'You never told me you had been here alone for five years.'

'I didn't think you liked older women.'

'I love them as long as they are you. You were lonely?'

'Hideously. Which is why I volunteered to go after you. Inskipp had another volunteer, but he broke his leg.'

'My darling — I'll bet I know how that happened!' She is not the blushing type, but she did lower her eyes at the thought.

'We are getting ahead in sequence,' Coypu said. 'But that is what happened. We traced you from 1975 to 1807 — and traced He and his minions as well. There was a loop in time there, an anomaly of some kind that eventually sealed itself off. We could tell that it was about to collapse with you sealed inside of it and succeeded at last in forcing enough power into the helix to penetrate the sealed time loop just before it went down. That is when Angelina went back with the coordinates for your next skip in time, the long twenty-thousand-year jump after He. You had to go after him because the time paths were there to prove that you had followed him. Though of course history was clear by that point, and we knew how it would all end.'

'You *knew*?' I asked, feeling I had missed the point somewhere.

'Of course. The entire nature of the attack was clear, though you all of course had to fulfill your destined roles.'

'Could you spell it out again? And slower.'

'Of course. You managed to destroy He's operation twice in the remote past and eventually reset his machine and sent him forward to the twilight days of Earth. Here he spent an immense amount of time, almost two hundred years, climbing his way to power and uniting all of the planet's resources. He was a genius, albeit a mad one, and could do this. He also remembered you, Jim, fading memories and half-insane ones after two hundred years, but he remembered enough to know you were the enemy. Therefore he launched a time war to destroy you before you could destroy him, trapping you as he thought on a planet about to be destroyed by atomic explosion. From there he returned to 1975 to attack the Corps. You came after him and he fled to 1807 to lay the time loop trap for you. I don't know where he planned to go from there, but his plans appear to have been altered, and he went instead twenty thousand years ahead.'

'I did that, altered the setting on his machine just before he left.'

'That is all there is to it. We can relax now that it is over, and I do believe I'll join you in that drink.'

'*Relax!*' The words emerged from my throat with a singularly nasty, grating sound. 'From what you have said it sounds like *I* started the whole attack on the Special Corps by altering the setting on the time-helix that sent He to the world where he launched his campaign to destroy the Corps.'

'That's one way of looking at it.'

'Is there any other? The way I see it He just bounces in a circle in time forever. Running from me, chasing me, running from me. . . . Arrrgh! When was he born? Where does he come from?'

'Those terms are meaningless in this sort of temporal relationship. He exists only within this time loop. If you wish to say it, though it is most imprecise, it would be fair to state that he was never born. The situation exists apart from time as we normally know it. Such as the fact that you returned here with the information to be sent to yourself about the settings on the atomic bombs. Where did this information come from originally? From yourself. So you sent it to yourself in order to send it to yourself to inform yourself about the settings on the bombs in order . . .'

'Enough!' I groaned, reaching for the bottle with trembling hand. 'Just mark the mission as being accomplished and put me in for a fat bonus.'

I refilled all the glasses and only when I came to Angelina's did I realize she was no longer present. She had slipped away without a word while I was suffering over having instigated the whole time war, and I was just beginning to miss her and wondered where she had gone when she returned

'They are fine,' she said.

'Who, who?' I said in my best owl imitation. But when I saw the narrowing of Angelina's eyes, I knew I had made a big mistake and I racked my time-trodden brain until understanding burst upon me. 'Who indeed! Ho-ho-ho! You must excuse the small joke. Who is fine, you say. Why, our twin, cherubic, gurgling babies are fine. With true maternal instinct you have rushed to their side.'

'They are here with me.'

'Well, wheel the pram in!'

'The babies,' she said as they entered, with what I detected as a strong note of irony.

They were going on six years of age, a little fact that I had neglected to remember. They moved easily, solid chaps with the disconcerting knack of walking in step with each other. Well muscled, their father's firm heritage, I am happy to say, with a tempering of their mother's looks.

'You've been away a long time, Dad,' one of them said.

'Not by choice, James. The universe isn't saved in a day.'

'I'm James, he's Bolivar. Welcome back.'

'Well, thanks.' Did I kiss them or what? They settled this by sticking out their hands, and I shook them each quite seriously. Good grips. This family thing was going to take some getting used to. Angelina beamed proudly, and I melted under that look and realized that it was all probably worth it.

'Angelina, I think you have finally convinced me. The joy of married life seem to be worth the price of giving up the happy and carefree occupation of free-lance thief. . . .'

'Thief is the correct word,' a nauseously familiar voice cried out. 'And crook, con man, blackmailer, briber, and more.' Inskipp stood in the doorway waving his florid face and a sheaf of papers in my direction. 'Five years I have been waiting for you, diGriz, and this time you are not getting away. No excuses like time wars now. You crook, you steal from your own buddies, *urggh!*'

He said *Urggh!* because Angelina had popped a sleep capsule under his nose, and he folded over while the boys – good reflexes there – stepped forward and eased him gently to the floor. Angelina relieved him of the sheaf of papers while he went by.

'After five years I need you more than this nasty old man does. Let's burn this file and steal a ship before he comes to. It will be months before he can find us, and by that time something else will have happened that will need straightening out badly, and he will have to put us back to work again. Meanwhile, we can have a lovely crooked second honeymoon.'

'Sounds great – but what about the boys? This is not the sort of trip one takes children on.'

'You're not leaving without us,' Bolivar said. Where had I seen that unshakable scowl before? In the mirror I guess. 'Where you go, we go. If it's a matter of money, we can pay our own way. See.'

I saw indeed as he extended a great bundle of credits that could pay his way right across the galaxy. But I also had a quick glimpse of a familiar golden wallet.

'Inskipp's money! You robbed that poor old man while you should have been helping him.' I flicked a quick look at James. 'And I suppose you will be able to tell time during the trip with his wristwatch that I see suddenly on your arm?'

'In their father's footsteps,' Angelina said proudly. 'Of course they come with us. And don't concern yourself with expenses, boys. Daddy can steal enough for all of us.'

It was too much. 'Why not!' I laughed. 'Here's to crime!' I raised my glass.

'Here's to time,' Coypu said, getting in the spirit of the thing.

'Here's to time crime!' we cried together and drained our glasses and broke them against the wall, and Coypu smiled avuncularly after us as we grabbed the children's hands and leaped lightly over Inskipp's snoring body and were out the door and away.

There's a bright and glorious universe out there, and we are going to enjoy every single bit of it.

# Sphere's Great Science Fantasy Series

All Sphere Books are available at your bookshop or newsagent, or can be ordered from the following address:

Sphere Books, Cash Sales Department,
P.O. Box 11, Falmouth, Cornwall.

Please send cheque or postal order (no currency), and allow 15p for the first book plus 5p per copy for each additional book ordered up to a maximum of 50p in U.K. or Eire. Overseas customers and B.F.P.O. please allow 20p for the first book and 10p per copy for each additional book.